ROD JONES

A NOVEL

Julia Paradise

SUMMIT BOOKS
New York

PUBLISHED BY SUMMIT BOOKS
A DIVISION OF SIMON & SCHUSTER, INC.
SIMON & SCHUSTER BUILDING
ROCKEFELLER CENTER
1230 AVENUE OF THE AMERICAS
NEW YORK, NY 10020
ORIGINALLY PUBLISHED IN AUSTRALIA BY MCPHEE
GRIBBLE PUBLISHERS IN ASSOCIATION WITH
PENGUIN BOOKS AUSTRALIA
SUMMIT BOOKS AND COLOPHON ARE TRADEMARKS OF
SIMON & SCHUSTER, INC.
DESIGNED BY EVE METZ
MANUFACTURED IN THE UNITED STATES OF AMERICA
1   3   5   7   9   10   8   6   4   2
LIBRARY OF CONGRESS CATALOGING IN PUBLICATION DATA
JONES, ROD
JULIA PARADISE.
I. TITLE.
PR9619.3.J694J85   1987   823   87-9945
ISBN 0–671–64663–X

For Chris

'In not a few cases, especially with women and where it is a case of elucidating erotic trains of thought, the patient's co-operation becomes a personal sacrifice, which must be compensated by some substitute for love . . .'

FREUD, *Psychotherapy of Hysteria.*

'Yes, stupidity consists in wanting to reach conclusions. We are a thread, and we want to know the whole cloth . . .'

FLAUBERT, *Letters.*

I

For several years a Scottish physician named Kenneth Ayres, popularly known as 'Honeydew' Ayres, had made his living from British expatriates in the International Settlement and, more particularly, from travellers stopping at the Astor House Hotel. A newcomer soon discovered that it was Honeydew because of the tobacco to which Ayres was addicted, Gallaher's Honeydew, and with which he was habitually filling his pipe. He might later hear whispers that there was another, more sinister source of this appellation.

In the spring of 1927 Ayres was thirty-four, and he made a considerable impression, not least because of his physical appearance. He was a huge man, some 250 pounds of him, wrapped uncomfortably into a starched collar and a blue serge suit. As he propelled his bulk from the Club and back to his hotel (his apartment on the third floor of the Astor House Hotel contained his consulting rooms) Ayres had to stop often, panting, for little rests. Rickshaw drivers had to struggle to get Ayres' weight into motion in a stream of Shanghai afternoon traffic.

You might have come across him at the Shanghai Club, to which he had been given a temporary membership which never quite became permanent and never quite expired, where he took up his allotted station half way down the Long Bar, in the ill-defined 'professional' ranks between the managers of business houses and the chief clerks. Or you might have found him upstairs, in one of the Club's deep leather armchairs with his brandy and post-prandial pipe engaged in talk with another young man, perhaps recently arrived in the East. For, apart from his bulk, the other thing which impressed one about Ayres was his conversation.

There were three things he loved to talk about: the City of Edinburgh, where he had spent his childhood and attended university; Sigmund Freud, under whose aegis Ayres had studied for a year in Vienna, and to whom, with his beard, Ayres bore a vague resemblance; and finally Ayres loved to talk about his countryman, J. M. Barrie, whose play 'Peter Pan' Ayres had seen in its premier season in 1904 as a lad of eleven up in London on a school holiday with his father, and in which he had promptly fallen in love with the actress who had played Wendy. (Barrie, entirely by the way, was to become Chancellor of Edinburgh University in 1930.)

Ayres was a success by any standards but his own. He was the son of a Scottish Colonel, and after school he had disappointed his father when he refused to join the regiment, turning instead to the study of medicine. It was while he was at university in Edinburgh that he first became interested in the treatment of nervous disorders.

He had spent the war in a military hospital in Here-
fordshire, where he had worked with the shellshocked.
In the nurses' station at the hospital he had met, then
married, a local girl. After the war, when her family,
solid Hereford gentry, began casting around the district
for a secure practice for him, his Caledonian restlessness
surfaced and for a time Ayres and his young wife travelled on the Continent. At first he had thoughts about
returning to the hospital to continue his work with the
nerve cases, but found himself instead, as effortlessly as
if it were an accident, spending the next year in Vienna,
enrolled as a member of Freud's graduate seminar.

Ayres was no genius, but he was a talented and con-
scientious student. He was overshadowed by the fiery
leading lights in Freud's circle, but even mediocre men
have their year, when their lives seem to take on a co-
herent direction—and that year in Vienna was Ayres'.
But he was about to be touched by something larger in
that winter of 1919: the Spanish Influenza epidemic.
His wife fell ill in Vienna and by the time they had returned to London she was dead.

For three years Ayres worked to the point of exhaustion to forget his grief; could not; and determined upon
that other classic palliative of the English—a steamship
ticket to the East. He sailed for Sydney, Australia, but
on a whim disembarked in Shanghai, and had been
there ever since.

Ayres had remained something of an outsider in
Shanghai. He spent his time at the Racing Club and in
the Long Bar, but among all his acquaintances there he
could count none as a friend. Socially, the British there

treated him with a polite and deferential suspicion. It was as though, with his appointment book full of the names of their wives and their daughters and their cases of petit mal, hysteria and the nervous collapses which followed broken love affairs, he had learned quite enough of their secrets, and they tended to exclude him.

In China, that pestilential dreamscape of suffering, he had no interest at all. He was not like those Englishmen who learned Mandarin and became scholars. The great thing about Shanghai for Ayres was its transience. Sitting at the Long Bar, or in the lobby of the Astor House Hotel, Ayres watched all those other foreign lives pass before him—the Englishwomen, even the healthy ones looking pallid and ill; the young adventure-seekers, the aspiring painters and writers on the cadge for a fiver; the fresh-faced young American missionaries who hoped, it seemed, to spread Christ in China by their sheer numbers. Some of these were insufferably boring. They were exhausted and fanatical and would talk of nothing else but Christianity and China in the same sentence. Others were frightened, the new ones whose only experience of a big city had been the three days they had spent in San Francisco before sailing, and who now, faced with the sights and sounds of eight million heathen people, suddenly felt their faith grow brittle and crack. They were sweaty-palmed and hollow-eyed, hoping the fear did not show on their faces. Sometimes they would turn up months later, broken men and raving women, reduced to being a part of the detritus of the city, and often victims of the various drugs of addiction.

It was into this foyer of the Astor House Hotel, late one Saturday afternoon, a woman flew, hesitated a moment, then turned and was gone behind the revolving glass panels of the still-spinning Berlin door as suddenly as she had arrived. Ayres caught just a glimpse of her face. Her eyes held him with their look of glittering disorientation. He saw that the desk clerk had noticed her too, suspecting perhaps that she might be a prostitute. All this took a second, no more; even as Ayres noticed her, she was on her way out.

A few minutes later, she was back again, this time clutching the arm of a reverend gentleman. He wore a hat, a celluloid collar, a dark suit, and carried his own cardboard suitcase, even though a porter had followed him through the door and was unoccupied. The woman was still panicky and disoriented. When the desk clerk, a Chinese, spoke to them she shrieked, felt behind her for one of the comfortable lobby sofas, sat down and promptly fell asleep, much to the desk clerk's puzzlement. The missionary gentleman shuffled shyly forward to the desk, still clutching his cardboard suitcase, to make his explanations.

Ayres followed all this with his usual detached interest and was surprised to see the desk clerk pointing in his direction; then to see the clergyman shuffling forward with his same uncertain gait and removing his hat.

He was a man of about fifty, Ayres judged, fair, balding with pale blue eyes. When he spoke up, Ayres discovered that his name was William Paradise, that he worked with the Methodist Missions in Shanghai and that, to judge from his harsh accent, he was an Australian.

'My wife,' he said slowly, 'has come in for a bit of a shock lately.'

Ayres did not appear to be very impressed. He threw the stub of the cigar he had been smoking into the brass spittoon, took out his bandana handkerchief, wiped a speck of phlegm from his mouth, inspected it, then put his handkerchief back in his pocket and began feeling for his pipe.

'I'm afraid she's become over-excited about things.' The man paused and blinked at Ayres. 'Things have been getting on top of her, rather. I'm afraid she has dropped her bundle altogether.'

Ayres looked across the hotel lobby at the calmly sleeping woman. She was small, plain, nondescript, of indeterminate age, dressed in a black woollen suit. The Reverend Paradise was saying, 'You will consent to examine her?' Ayres found his pipe and examined the blackened tar on its bowl with apparent distaste.

'You had better bring her upstairs. See if you can wake her. Or, if you like, I'll get a couple of boys to load her into a barrow and take her up in the luggage lift.'

The other man said apologetically, 'My wife's case has perplexed several physicians before yourself.' He added as an afterthought, 'I don't expect you to perform any miracles.'

Ayres' rooms were on the third floor of the building, connected with the ground by a notoriously unreliable lift, an iron cage which groaned and shuddered on its cables and pulleys even when it did work. It was the bane of Ayres' existence: as a heavy man he hated stairs. On this particular Saturday afternoon, already past the hour when Ayres customarily took his tea, the lift was working, although the lift porter was nowhere to be seen. He passed the little wooden alcove with its sliding window and saw the boy inside wrapped in a blanket, asleep in his chair. He climbed the three steps to the lift landing, opened the iron concertina door and ushered the missionary and his suitcase into the lift. The door closed and he turned the handle. The cables shuddered and whined and they began to ascend. As they did so, Ayres caught a glimpse of two porters loading the comatose little woman onto a wooden barrow.

At first the Reverend Paradise seemed uncomfortable imparting the intimate details of his wife's illness to a stranger but, once he had begun his story and got into his stride, he impressed Ayres as a kindly, intelligent man whose main concern was that his wife should get well again. As he spoke he nodded his head from time to time as if to reassure himself of the truth of his words. Ayres was able to piece together the following story.

During her first year in this country the young woman had been troubled by cravings for sleep during the daytime. She had formerly been extremely energetic in carrying out her teaching duties. In the course of these attacks of drowsiness she had taken to talking in snatches of German. As a child she had heard her father speak German at home, although to all intents and purposes English was her native tongue. Her husband spoke no German. These cravings for rest were accompanied by sleeplike states at odd times throughout the day— 'waking daydreams' the Reverend Paradise called them. Even during meals and conversations with visitors to the mission the missionary's wife would literally fall asleep on her feet.

On a long journey through the Interior on an evangelistic mission with a group of English teaching and medical missionaries his wife had begun to suffer from certain disturbances of her vision. The group had as one of their number an English doctor, who administered sedatives. But when this course of treatment was withdrawn, the disturbances of vision returned, and he called them by another name: hallucinations.

Put simply, she began to see animals which weren't really there. This zoöpsia took many forms: a tribute to the imagination, had they been deliberate invention. She saw mice, rats, insects, snakes—her imagination seemed to select the classically loathsome creatures. One of her most persistent hallucinations was a small brightly patterned snake moving across the floor in the periphery of her vision. Her zoöpsia was accompanied by a terror of real animals. The mere touch of fur, even in a coat, caused her nausea. Her pet miniature dog, which formerly she had fawned over, now revolted her and she had killed it with a walking stick in a fit of terror.

A serious problem, in the light of their Christian mission in this country, was that the patient developed a virulent sinophobia, referring to the local people, even the Christian Chinese with whom they worked, as dogs. She also began to suffer from serious hallucinations of fire. She felt that she actually was, or was about to be, trapped inside a burning building. These hallucinations consumed her, threw her into paroxysms of terror to the point where she could smell the smoke, hear the crackle of the flames and the screams of the other victims, and feel the heat of the fire on her hands and face.

She had returned with her husband to the little mission school twenty miles outside Shanghai where they presently lived and worked. She had become abusive even towards their European colleagues. She was an embarrassment to her husband, but a cross he had to bear. She was deliberately rude to visitors to the mission and flew into terrible rages with her husband. She threw tantrums in which she banged her head against the wall, ripped the buttons off her clothing and exposed herself.

Her dementia worsened to such an extent that she began to live more and more in her room. She lived in a kind of twilight world pretty much divorced from the daily life of the mission school. She lived the sheltered life of an invalid and became increasingly dependent on medication. She alternated between periods of torpor and flashes of brilliant hallucination during which she would sometimes write late into the night in her penny notebooks, the common paper-covered books into which the pupils used to copy their exercises.

During these 'creative' periods she would sometimes leave her room and roam the mission grounds and the countryside around the mission in an agitated condition. At other times she would catch the train to Shanghai and wander night and day through the dangerous and unsanitary Chinese quarters with her camera—one of her delusions was that she considered herself to be a 'serious' photographer. It was during these periods that her behaviour was more likely to be violent and anti-social, and she became a regular visitor to the cells of the police precincts of the International Settlement. She had embarked upon one of these escapades the previous evening and the Reverend Paradise had walked the streets all that morning looking for her. He had finally found her, in her present pitiful and exhausted condition, in a workingman's tea-house; whence he had brought her here.

The Reverend William Paradise finished his story with a kind of pitiful exhaustion of his own. He wiped his handkerchief across his flushed pink forehead. Ayres looked back at him from his armchair with a mixture of mild enquiry and contempt. 'I might point out,' he said quietly, 'that cases such as these are common to the point of banality here.'

A whimper of disbelief escaped from the clergyman. 'Like my wife's, you say?'

'I've seen hospital wards full of neurotic English-women, many of them victims of their husbands' ambitions in the colonial services. Some of them are just gin-soaked biddies in there to dry out and to have a bit of a rest.'

The other man said in his quiet, pleading voice, 'We are Methodists.'

Ayres looked back at him, a hint of amusement in the shape of his mouth through his beard. He said, 'We put it down to the East. Sooner or later the women are shipped home and I daresay that in many cases simple homesickness is as good an explanation as any.'

'And this is the category into which you are putting my wife?'

'Not at all. I simply wished to point out that I have seen quite severe cases of dementia among European women here in China and in the end the cure was as simple as a steamship ticket home.'

'Our home is here, Ayres. These are now our people. We have our mission.'

Ayres looked at him and made no attempt to disguise his contempt. The other man saw this and went on quickly, 'You will consent to examine her, though?'

'I'll examine her.' Ayres tried to smile, but the effect only added to his visitor's disquiet. 'As you said, no miracles. You go downstairs and have some tea and I'll see what I can do for her. Try a piece of the strudel cake. They do serve excellent teas here.'

Julia Paradise was awake. She lay on his leather Ottoman and looked around the strange room in which she found herself. A range of expressions formed on her face: a scowl, a frown, a brief relaxation into her former languor, then a look of utterly pathetic dejection. When she spoke—a word here and there in answer to Ayres' questions—her voice slurred as she salivated, and now and then the saliva dribbled uncontrollably from the corner of her mouth.

She was not a pretty woman. Her dark hair was at once short and untidy and her eyes were made unnaturally large by the thinness of her face. Her skin was pale, anemic and unhealthy looking. Her nervous little figure was emaciated, as though it had never filled out from girlhood, and she was apparently breastless.

It was immediately obvious to Ayres from the jerky agitation of her movements and from her habitual relapse into a masklike apathetic expression that she was indeed suffering from a serious nervous condition. The mask contorted from time to time without warning into spasms of *tics douloureux*. Her hands were particularly thin, the skin stretched tightly over the bones of her knuckles and her fingers were reddened and scaly with what looked like dermatitis. Her face was so emaciated with its dark eyes, stark cheekbones and cropped hair, that Ayres asked himself whether there might not be something organically wrong with her, whether or not she might after all be the victim of a wasting disease. He had formed the conclusion from her husband's account that she was an hysteric; an hypothesis in which the physician who had previously examined her apparently concurred.

Then Ayres smiled in grim recognition. He went over to his desk and slowly, methodically unpacked his surgical bag. He was not so much of a specialist that he did not have to cope with the common run of complaints among the guests staying at the hotel, the gastric upsets and diarrhea, the sore throats and influenza that were a lesser man's bread and butter—as well as his occasional forages into the exotic gardens of the mind. He sorted through the contents of his bag—the stethoscope, the blood pressure apparatus, the large chrome-plated syringe and the box of needles, and the other box containing the ampoules of morphine.

The little woman watched him, bright-eyed now, perched on the edge of the Ottoman, wiping her chin from time to time with the back of her hand. He walked over and helped her remove the shabby black woollen jacket of her suit, then rolled up the sleeve of her blouse.

He had guessed right. The inside of her right arm was covered with puncture marks. He watched her, but she was looking down at her arm and her face showed no emotion. Then, as he walked over to his desk to get the syringe and ampoule, he heard the noise she was making, a kind of deep grizzling growl in her throat—

exactly the noise of a sick animal whimpering. A sob, a sniffle, the sound of her sucking in her saliva. He took up the spirit bottle and a piece of cotton waste. She stretched her arm out, waiting.

'Not today,' he said. 'We'll give that arm of yours a bit of a rest, I think.' He lifted the hem of her skirt over her knees, and above the plump stocking rolls on each thigh. He rubbed the flesh with the alcohol, then, holding up the syringe, pricked the tip of the needle through the taut rubber skin stretched over the ampoule and drew back the plunger. She winced as he inserted the needle into her clean white thigh.

It seemed that Ayres was finally to be left alone that afternoon. His rooms had a dark, still, empty feeling. He was at a loose end, vaguely annoyed: he usually allowed himself the Englishman's Saturday half-holiday. Ayres walked back into his study, a large room at the front of his apartment overlooking the street. In one corner was an ornate amber and rose stained-glass window— an oddity in an hotel room, he had always thought. The little fireplace was surrounded with tiles to match the amber in the glass. A lonely Saturday afternoon smell pervaded his rooms. There was the smell of stale furniture polish, and the faint tang of oranges which made him think, for some reason, of the Reverend William Paradise.

Ayres drew the blinds, then the curtains, then switched on the two standard lamps whose glow surged and faded unsteadily with the unreliable current of Shanghai's electricity supply. Then he lowered his bulk into his winter fireside chair, an oversized armchair with

a carved wooden back, which was upholstered in bur-
gundy velvet and striped quilted damask. He had also
turned on his green-shaded desk lamp, although he had
no intention of sitting at his desk where substantial bun-
dles of mail and English-language newspapers and pe-
riodicals were awaiting him in piles.

The door of his study opened and his Chinese boy
appeared, carrying a tray with coffee. When the boy
went out Ayres reached across to pour from the pot, then
settled back in his shirtsleeves and waistcoat. He sipped
the coffee, preoccupied by something. Perhaps he had a
headache, but his face bore the marks of a man trying to
think of something he had forgotten more than of any
sudden pain. A vein beat in his temple, a gentle persistent throb, as though reminding him of something.

Presently the boy came in again, this time with Ayres'
smoking things. There was a small spirit lamp, two pipes
and an intricately carved jade box. Without a word the
pipes were prepared. The boy took a small ball of the
sticky opium and rolled it between his finger and thumb,
then speared it on the needle and baked it in the flame
of the spirit lamp until it crackled. As Ayres bent forward
with the pipe held to his mouth, the boy set the needle
into the pipe. The pipe crackled, and Ayres drew the
smoke down into his lungs.

The boy made up the other pipe in the same way as
the first, then left. Ayres smoked it and settled back in
his chair. A long time passed. His thoughts did not want
to break his trance by speaking to him. He felt a thought
rise up in him then fade before he could recognize it.
He felt that he was on the point of making a crucial
confession to himself, but that he was holding himself

back from such an irrevocable step as an admission of guilt: like a murderer might feel, for instance.

Twice or three times a week it was Ayres' habit to venture out into the city to visit his painter friends. The latest of these artists was named Morgan, a young graduate of the Slade School in London, and a fellow Scot. When Ayres had first met him he was living like an animal, hungry, in a bare unheated room in the Chinese quarter, where he slept on a mat on the stone floor and did his paintings—when he could afford to buy paints—on the sides of old packing cases. Ayres, playing the patron, had installed the man in more suitable accommodation in the old American Concession, paid him a small weekly allowance and the fees for his models.

These models were invariably Chinese girls barely out of childhood. Indeed both men might have been shocked had they known their actual ages. They were prostitutes whom Ayres himself procured from a house in the Bubbling Well Road. After the painter had made use of her all day, sometimes Ayres went to make use of her at night. As these girls were always thin and small, the sexual contrast with his own gross size was a painful one to contemplate, and what he preferred. In the artist's rooms at night he always took them in the same position: from behind. All such girls were in his mental notation, 'Wendies', with their wispy boy-like figures, unformed breasts, bony hips and slender arms.

Ayres recognized this in himself indulgently. He knew well Freud's remark that 'some perverse trait or other is seldom absent from the sexual life of normal people'.

Afterwards he sometimes bought both artist and model a drink and something to eat in one of the nightclubs of the quarter. It had been there, outside the building where Morgan lived in Szechuan Road, just down from the post office, that he saw Willy Paradise's little wife, late that night after her strange Saturday afternoon consultation.

He had just put on his hat and coat and had come down the stairs. It was as though she had been standing at the door, trying to decide whether to go in, when Ayres had appeared. She turned quickly away and started walking, wrapped in her thick overcoat, clutching her basket, bundling her way along the street.

It was nearly midnight and the street was deserted. In the doorways of the post office families of beggars huddled together out of the wind. Now the little woman was running with such a sense of urgency that, although the beggars followed her with their eyes, none bothered to approach her.

Ayres walked after her twenty, then fifty, then a hundred yards behind. She did not turn. She passed eventually into the French Concession and still Ayres followed her. The French policemen did not emerge from their patrol post. Ayres saw the shadows of their heads moving in the light against the frosted glass.

Julia Paradise had entered a region of tenements, rat-infested boarding houses where the sewage ran open into the streets. Between these buildings even more temporary accommodations had been constructed out of flattened kerosene tins, packing cases and any other materials that could be scrounged. Every few months a detachment of French soldiers moved through the Concession pulling

26

down these shanties and turning the wretches who inhabited them out onto the streets. But that night the only noise which disturbed the residents of the slum from their sleep was the sound of a woman's running footsteps, and even further behind her, the heavy tread and straining breath of Dr Ayres.

He had come out onto one of the main thoroughfares of the Concession—he thought it was the Avenue Edouard VII but couldn't be sure in the absence of streetlamps. This was not his usual territory. The tumbledown buildings had given way to blocks of apartments and bigger houses. From the dim windows of the houses came sudden snatches of conversation, a song, an argument, the cry of a child. The shop-fronts were covered with sheets of corrugated iron, the more prosperous establishments barred with heavy iron grilles. When Ayres turned the next corner she was gone.

He knew she must have disappeared into one of those low dark buildings which had been divided by greedy landlords into warrens of single rooms in which often two or three families were crammed.

He walked back along that street of evil aspect, feeling cold and alone and frightened. The buildings all looked the same to him now, and the occasional window high up lit with the weak wobbly light of a kerosene lamp was not reassuring. He could not completely get rid of the feeling that the figure of the woman had lured him into some danger, or an ambush, that at any moment now someone would step out of the shadows in front of him.

There was nothing he could do but quicken his pace along the street to the comparative safety of the French patrol post, find a taxi, and begin the chore of haggling a fare back to the Astor House. He rapped on the window of the first car on the rank. The driver suddenly shot up, startled from sleep, thinking Ayres was one of the French policemen, perhaps.

He saw her several times around the city after that, always dressed in the same old raincoat, the same scarf tied over her head, the shopping basket on her arm. A casual observer who happened to know of her vocation might have assumed that she was ministering to the poor of the city, arranging food and shelter for the derelict.

Usually she was far away, or sufficiently caught up in the movement of the crowds not to have to acknowledge Ayres. Only once did he see her in the company of another person. It was on a Sunday afternoon. They were strolling arm in arm along the Bund in the sunshine. Her tall companion wore a man's hat and carried a briefcase and from across the road Ayres assumed it was her husband. Then, as the couple crossed and walked towards him, he saw she was a woman whose expression was serious under the brim of her hat. They passed close enough for him to see the silver crosses glinting on the collars of their blouses. He followed them idly as far as the grim building which housed the Y.W.C.A. and the Women's Institute, successor to the Anti-Footbinding League. They climbed the steps and disappeared into the gloom inside.

Then, early one morning when Ayres was still in his evening clothes from a party at the Black Cat night-club and making his way home in the fresh air, he spotted the Paradise woman strolling through the vegetable markets.

He was standing quite near her when she looked up and saw him. She jumped with the recognition, thrust her head down and began to push her way through the shoppers, looking wretched in the raincoat and scarf she always wore. Ayres had drunk enough that night to steel his determination to catch up with her this time, and he shouldered ruthlessly through the crowds of early morning shoppers. When she saw how close he was the woman stopped and waited, and he could see the strain in her eyes.

She had her basket on her arm just as though she had come among these women of poor Chinese families to buy her vegetables. Then he caught a glimpse of a rather expensive-looking camera inside it. She saw him looking and snatched the basket away.

'I photograph,' she said simply.

Yet it was not such a simple thing to say. Surely one said—'I *take* photographs'? But the little missionary woman had used the verb strongly, almost defiantly. Then her eyes had become vague and unfocused again and she looked away from him, shifting the weight from one foot to the other. There remained between them unspoken her ghostly disappearance outside Morgan's rooms. And Ayres was still drunk and determined enough to want to exact the revenge of an explanation to the full. He compounded her discomfort by asking her to join him for breakfast.

Perhaps it was her embarrassment, or perhaps she

couldn't think of a plausible excuse to refuse. In either case, she accepted. She said that she would join him—but only for a bowl of tea.

Now breakfast was of custom an occasion for Ayres. He liked to build his day on a foundation of all varieties and combinations of offal and eggs. He was especially partial to a bit of liver or kidney with his chops and bacon to set off the blandness of the eggs. To breakfast on a bowl of China tea was inconceivable to this man, yet he followed her meekly through the crowds, in his silk top hat, tails and white silk scarf.

Dotted among those market streets were numerous tea houses. They were not visited by Europeans normally, and were rough and ready shops designed to give fast service and to send the workingman on his way. But the missionary's wife seemed to have one tea shop in particular in mind. As they entered, the coolies seated along the wooden benches with their tea bowls and cigarettes, stared at them. Just as incongruous were they, with Ayres in his evening clothes, as those coolies might have been if they had arrived in their singlets and padded jackets to take high tea in the dining-room of the Astor House Hotel.

Julia Paradise did not seem much inclined to talk with her tea. She looked around the mean surroundings—the grimy green paintwork of the tables and benches, the steam from the urn dripping down the window in rivulets, the sawdust on the floor and everywhere the thick pall of cheap tobacco. Her eyes met Ayres' from time to time and—this surprised him—she seemed to be laughing. The workingmen on their benches were all silent, watching the interlopers with fear and suspicion:

the devil himself might have walked in. Perhaps the woman was amused to have lured Ayres in his evening clothes into this monkey cage. Ayres said, after a while, 'If you'd rather we left and took our tea in more congenial surroundings—'

She shook her head once. 'It isn't that.'

'The breakfasts they give at my hotel are very good.'

'I'm sure they are.' There was irony in her expression now, and her prominent eye-teeth were bared, but whether in humour or in malice he couldn't tell. He formed his next sentence carefully. 'You know my hotel, I think. You visited me there several weeks ago.'

She seemed not to have understood. He continued, 'That was before I saw you that night outside Morgan's.'

She listened to his statement of the fact drily, unmoved. She did not deny it; how could she? She lowered her eyes but immediately shot them back to meet his gaze, the defiant expression which Ayres already thought of as characteristic. He feared for a moment that she would demand to know by what right he had followed her. But she went on quickly, 'I spend some nights in the city. Looking for subjects for my photographs.'

'In the dark?'

'Yes.' She did not condescend to explain further.

He said slyly, 'You know Morgan, then?'

Ayres noticed that some of the old physical symptoms of strain had begun to creep into her face. The tic was back in her cheek, along the edge of one nostril. She began to speak in a voice that had taken on the tinge of a German accent again. Halting and lighting on an imaginary object, she paused from what she was saying, stifled a gulp of terror, and Ayres knew that she was seeing her

31

animals again. At one point, looking at a fantastic creature rather than Ayres, she accused, 'You killed her.'

Ayres was at a disadvantage without his medical bag. Clearly, she was hallucinating, rocking back and forth in the wooden chair. He knew he had to get her out of there in a hurry.

The Chinese workingmen had left and others had come in and taken their places. Their curiosity in seeing Europeans—even such bizarre Europeans who wore evening clothes to a market tea house—soon palled, and they paid no attention to the woman's antics. There was nothing Ayres could do. He slapped a couple of copper coins onto the wooden table and, striding around behind her, lifted her bodily from the chair and slung her over his shoulder. Now the Chinese customers followed his movements with an intense curiosity. As he lifted her the basket toppled over and her camera rattled across the hard stone floor in the sawdust. One of the onlookers picked up the black object suspiciously, then the basket, and placed it into Ayres' free hand. In this way he walked out of the smoky gloom of the tea shop and into the crowds on the pungent sunlit early-morning streets.

That morning in his rooms at the Astor House Hotel Ayres discovered the most suggestible patient he had ever come across in his life. None of the ladies in Vienna whose cases he had studied, not even the legendary successes of the Master himself, had provided a subject whose other, 'hidden' self was so accessible through hypnosis, or so discernibly opposite to the face she presented to the world.

Not that Ayres was taken in by the more excessive

and ludicrous claims made in some quarters for hypnosis as a therapy. Hypnosis, as he had learned to practise it in Vienna, began with touch, with a laying on of hands. This proved to be his first indication of the extraordinary suggestibility of Julia Paradise. He began by massaging her trapezius muscles, down the back of the neck and along her shoulders. These muscles were in spasm and bunched up tightly. Several times she opened her eyes and asked in English for morphine. After a period of massage he allowed her to sleep for half an hour as a relief from her anxieties. Ayres took this time to have his bath drawn and to change into ordinary day clothes. He ordered coffee and eggs to be sent up and ate his breakfast in his consulting room, still watching over her.

When he saw that the woman was awake and comparatively relaxed, he encouraged her to talk about her childhood in Australia. He questioned her gently, tempting her to answer. He allowed her talk to wander and did not interrupt to get her back onto her track. Gradually, over some hours, she built up for him a picture so vivid and disturbingly at odds with the details of her early life her husband had given him, that Ayres did not believe she was hypnotized in the accepted sense of the word. He put down as mere hallucinations these wild and often obscene flights of fancy into her world of the animals. He concluded that under hypnosis she was actually 'speaking her dreams' as they occurred in her subconscious mind. At the same time she was conscious enough to be talking to him.

Later, when she was fully awake, she insisted that her childhood on her father's plantation in northern Queensland, Australia, had been settled and happy. She told him that she had been a serious and religious girl, and that it had seemed wholly appropriate that she marry a preacher. Then Ayres told her some of the things she had said while under hypnosis. She did not slap his face, although initially she looked as though she might. In the end she simply said that she did not believe him.

She agreed to return in three days' time; by now the case had truly drawn Ayres' interest. Before she left she mentioned that soon after her arrival in China she had suffered from a serious bout of illness which had necessitated a stay in the American Hospital. 'I nearly died then, you know,' she told him. This claim of hers of being mortally ill was contradicted after an hour's struggle with the Shanghai telephone system. The American Hospital's records confirmed that she had been admitted the year before last for three days, with an entirely routine case of gastro-enteritis.

Every Tuesday she travelled by train into the city and in the afternoons she visited Ayres' rooms and let him hypnotize her. He was astounded by the stock of imaginative products she unloaded while in a relaxed state. He regularly administered doses of morphine to help induce sleep, and sleep was preceded by a state of intoxication which lasted several hours. Sometimes he used these periods of intoxication to encourage the description of her hallucinations in detail. It seemed to afford the woman tremendous relief to verbalize these frightful images and thereby render them harmless, and she invariably woke from these sessions feeling refreshed. But something else was happening: Ayres was convinced that he was finally being allowed to approach the psychic events of her childhood which lay at the root of her hysterical illness.

She was not continually hallucinating. She was sometimes relaxed enough to talk without prompting about the little details of daily life at the mission school. Their mission was devoted to the ideal of giving girl children a Christian education. This activity had engendered opposition from some of the more traditional local families: it was not so very long before this time that footbinding had been legally practised. Julia Paradise talked about two or three of the girls she had taught the year before who had been withdrawn from the school by their families under pressure from others. One of the girls had died, apparently—in any case it upset her to speak of it and Ayres wisely desisted in his questions.

But during relatively happy conversations she was still plagued by hallucinations. Even as she recited for him a poem—she had several of Keats and one by Coleridge learned by heart—the animals lay in wait for her in the corners of Ayres' consulting rooms. She would hesitate a moment in the line she was reciting, and Ayres came to interpret this pause to mean that she had seen a mouse move under the bed. At odd moments she fell into 'sleeplike states' and Ayres became as used to these as anyone else who knew her. One afternoon she suddenly broke off from what she had been saying to complain of a large toad sitting squarely in the middle of the rug in front of them. They even managed to laugh about it.

But more often the stress of coping with her hallucinations, of sifting through her perceptions, so to speak, to find which were real and which imagined, became too much for her and the old terror returned and with it an exacerbation of her hysterical symptoms.

She described over the weeks these visions of the animals to Ayres in great detail. Delicate, whip-like snakes 'the colour of red earth'; toads 'as big as a man's hand, horribly pale and skin-coloured'. Any sudden or unexpected movement in her peripheral vision—such as a curtain flapping in the breeze—had the power to turn itself into an animal for her.

These neurotic symptoms were, of course, complicated by her narcotic addiction, which Ayres did his best to control. Sometimes she was able to prevail upon him to let her have an extra ampoule beyond her ration of five grains a day against the possibility of a very bad night. But she had apparently found another source of the stuff, and there were Tuesdays when he could see by the languidness of her movements, the apathy of her expression that his specified dosage had been exceeded. Ayres assumed that her husband was still ignorant of this matter; a state of affairs which suited Ayres, who knew only too well how false the non-addict's view of addiction can be. Besides, she was a reasonably well-adjusted addict and Ayres was utterly convinced by now that it was not her addiction which lay at the root of her problem.

Even under the influence of morphine she still had the capacity to talk lucidly and intelligently, and it was when she was physically groggy like this, with her hair tousled and eyes wild, she exercised upon Ayres a grotesque kind of sexual attraction. In fact her slim childish figure had begun to interest him a great deal. Her unre-

36

markable freckled little face became dominated by her
eyes, which glittered in her head as she tried to make
him understand the intensity of her hallucinations. Com-
monly, their conversations held an element of ironic
teasing.

'How do you know these animals are not really there?'
she asked.

'No-one else sees them.'

'But what if they're really here and it's just that at the
moment neither you nor I can see them?'

'Nonsense!'

'But isn't it possible that the animals are really there,
but that they're hiding in order to trick me? You will at
least admit the possibility?'

'No!' he laughed. 'They only want to annoy you.
They have nothing against me.'

'No!' When she laughed her serious worried face
changed completely. She took on the look of a young
girl about to participate in some treat.

'Or perhaps you're not looking hard enough to find
them.'

'Only mad people think like that. Not doctors.'

'How else are you to understand the complaints of
your patients?' She paused, then added, 'I never think
of you having other patients, apart from me.'

She looked at him intently, her lips pressed together.
She had begun to sweat profusely, even though the day
was not particularly hot.

'Are you seeing the animals now?'

She silently mouthed 'No' but the look of abstraction,
of rapt intensity, inclined Ayres to disbelief.

Whenever Ayres questioned her closely about her

childhood the invisible barrier went up between them. It was not that she didn't co-operate—she spoke of her childhood in such vivid and far-fetched detail that Ayres thought always that she was hallucinating.

Then, just when he felt that he had reached a dead end in the case, one afternoon when she was quite relaxed and fully conscious, she said something to him in German. He remembered of course that her father's language in her childhood had been German, and that her husband had said she had spoken in German during the initial stages of her breakdown.

Ayres himself had become fluent in the language during his year in Vienna, so he understood perfectly what she had said: *'Also sie haben noch einen Heizer geschickt.'* Instinctively, Ayres feigned ignorance and replied vaguely, 'Eh?' She laughed, and went on to talk in English about something quite unrelated. Ayres couldn't help feeling that she was teasing him, and it occurred to him that perhaps she had been teasing him in other respects. But the fact that she had said the word, *Heizer*, fireman, remained in his mind. They'd sent a fireman. It seemed a clue to something. When he had pretended not to understand he had caught her looking at him, momentarily but unmistakably, with something like contempt.

She was still a long way from being cured of her troubles. On occasions she would appear at his door in a state of near panic. Without a word of greeting she would take off her coat and lie down on Ayres' Ottoman and wait irritably for the massage and the soothing words to begin. When she was tense like this, the words flew out of her—her hallucinations, her old animal phobias, her affection for a dead pupil, little things about Willy and the mission spilled out, jumbled up—nightmare and reality together. It was as though her mind were a pressure cooker full of such fears and images, that the whole lot might explode disastrously in her head without the relief of her weekly visit to Ayres, and another of her hysterical breakdowns occur.

The animals, cunning creatures, lay in wait for her mercilessly: the toads and snakes pursued her wherever she went from the mission school. The starched white sheets and crisp counterpane of Ayres' bed, the cream-painted bars of the bedstead, were no defence. One Tuesday she awoke after her morphine injection only to find a bloated toad sitting on her stomach, watching her. Many was the time she looked up from a book in Ayres' sitting room to see the skinny brown snakes writhing in silent scrutiny across the parquet floor. Ayres feared that she might become a constant living rebuke to science.

But at last, after many weeks, something began to happen. The patient's spirits seemed suddenly to improve, her general health was better and her hallucinations troubled her less often. She was able to engage more fully in the life of the mission school. She reported that her husband had allowed her to resume part of her teaching duties. On fine mornings she took the girls out of doors, reciting poetry under the mulberry tree in the mission garden. She even began to talk of plans for a short holiday. With her mind thus occupied she slept better, and she had apparently ceased her nocturnal wanderings about the city.

Only with the doctor did Julia Paradise continue to explore the world of her illness. In his dark room with the shutters closed, the line of his pipe smoke drifting up to meet the flickering blades of the fan in the ceiling, she was confident, even brazen. She began to impart quite deliberately to Ayres the details of her childhood which had so profoundly disturbed and excited him in 'hallucinated' form. Now she began coldly and methodically to build up for him a picture of her father, Joachim Johannes.

She lay in the doctor's bed, relaxed in the crook of his big pale arm; or turned away from him facing the wall, her eyes open, shifting her head on the pillow from time to time to gauge his reaction; later she climbed over him, kneeling astride his bloated stomach so he could look at her flat little chest and dark nut-like nipples. And all the time she talked, and talked, as though she would never stop.

It was in this way their regular Tuesday afternoon adultery began.

When she was thirty and in the grip of that mad music she sang to 'Honeydew' Ayres, Julia often wandered back to the Duck River region in Northern Australia where she had spent her childhood. In particular she liked to dwell on that morning when she had drifted calmly away from her horror-struck father on the roof of the bawdy house at Mem.

Her father, Joachim Johannes, a German-born explorer and naturalist whose feats have now fallen into obscurity, was often away from the big wooden house on the marshy land on the edge of the rainforest he and his English wife had inherited. Julia had been born in that house and she had vivid memories from the earliest age of the sound and sight of the mosquitoes rising in clouds at dusk. She remembered how the Kanaka and Chinese servants chattered in their strange mixture of tongues as they bustled the little Julia indoors and rigged the mosquito nets over the big casement windows. Even then, before her mother's illness and death, the nursery maids and governesses blighted Julia's existence.

When he was at home and not scaling mythical western peaks or traversing southern oceans, her father was on the brown Duck River, rowing barechested in the tropical sun with his sketchbooks and a wicker-covered jug of wine in the bows. In those hours she spent with her half-tipsy father in the flat-bottomed boat it had seemed to the child that the purpose of her life had already been accomplished.

It had been her father who had first taken her down to the wide slow river in the buggy, who initiated her into the world of the wild river animals. In the boat, straining the great muscles of his chest and arms as he rowed, he took time to point out the various species among the teeming bird life and the dull ribbons of snakes on the brown banks. It was through her father, 'Doktor' Johannes, an immense man with his little alpine mountaineer's hat and his cigar clamped firmly between his teeth, that she first developed her love for the river life. Her father was blamed, first by his wife, then by the women he employed and seduced, for making their young charge such an incorrigible tomboy.

Years later, her father stood with Tina Terrina on the roof of the Hotel Continental in Mem the morning of the great flood, while the buildings and the animal population of the upcountry farms raced past them. He was astounded as he watched his daughter manipulating the tiller and expertly dodging the larger tree trunks and the bloated carcases of pigs, sheep, and cattle which had made their way downriver to the delta and the mangrove country and, eventually, to the sea.

• • •

Julia was tiny and the world huge. She had come inside early for her lesson. She loved her father's study with its leather chairs, the big redwood desk and the walls full of books. But more than this she was fascinated by his laboratory which adjoined it through a door of frosted glass. It was in there her father practised his taxidermy and where he kept all his instruments and his trays of geological samples. Even the strange, awful smells attracted her: formaldehyde, ammonia and methylated spirit. She loved above all else to observe her father at work in there, to watch him with his white apron over his waistcoat and cravat as he cast his scientific spells over matter animate and inanimate.

Sometimes, such was his reputation among the local people, she had barged in and found him peering into the mouth of a whiskery islands man suffering from toothache; or miraculously producing a baby from one of the three fat De Vooer sisters who lived at the edge of the little settlement and who all wore identical straw hats with veils and tissue paper roses on them.

Door handles were unreachable and she could hardly lift her father's black Bible from the lectern. Today she wanted him to read to her but the study was empty and there was only the smell of the leather chairs and the light coming through from the other side of the frosted glass door. Here she saw the shadow of her father bending over something inside—bending over the washbasin, or brushing his beard in the mirror, perhaps.

She stood in the dim study for a long time puzzling over the groans she could hear and watching his bending shadow at work on the other side of the frosted glass.

She was putting off the delicious moment when she would walk in and he would show his surprise and pleasure, then turn back to his work at the table and benches.

The little girl in the neat pinafore, her father's heavy black Bible hugged to her hollows, drew closer to the frosted glass door. The shadows continued to move. As she touched the door and it opened she felt very tired. The book slipped from her hands and was lost somewhere and she entered the room slowly as if she was moving through the warm landscape of sleep.

It came upon her so suddenly that she was amazed she hadn't time to shout out against it, or even to shut her eyes. Yet now as she heard herself speak, her voice was very old, as though another were saying it: 'Papa?'

A glimpse of their servant woman, Dolly Hang, full lips, squinting, smooth stripes of scar tissue across her cheeks. Pain and compassion for the child on her face. She was bending forwards over the scrubbed wooden table with her skirt around her belly, buttocks bared. Her father, fully dressed and maintaining his decorum in every way except that his trouser flies were unbuttoned, was in the act of penetrating her from behind. Her father looked down at the woman, whose face had always frightened Julia, as though surprised to find her there, then looked at his daughter at the door.

The girl turned and ran with her amazing discovery into the garden, where her mother was buried. Blank blue afternoon greeted her. Benign, mundane day, lacking in any sense of outrage. Wet washing flapped on the clothesline like laughter.

'Douglas!' the child called. 'Douglas come quickly!'

As if by some trick of her father's time-lapse photography she watched him advance. Douglas Hang leaned forward as he ran from the vegetable garden, carrying the spade he had been using to dig potatoes. Its sharpened head flashed in the sunlight. He swept the spade from side to side low through the air, and in his effortless jerky progress from one posture to the next he was suddenly at her side. But something was wrong. Here was Dolly Hang out in the garden where she was still bent over with her buttocks bared. All the members of the Hang family and their long dead ancestors in ceremonial dress were stepping forward in unison with the same jerky steps, a dance well-rehearsed, the skeleton of a dragon which only the child could see.

There was exquisite timing in their steps, they moved magically, they smiled, these ghosts, and showed by their smiles that they knew she was there. Smiles of unmistakable recognition. It seemed strange to Julia that they did not attempt to speak to her in language. The blur of ancestral motion focused again into Douglas Hang at her side. She heard the water from the pump splashing into the iron bucket; then she felt the cold water on her cheeks.

Next she was staring up into Dolly Hang's face. At first she could not understand how the woman could be out here in the yard under the bunya-bunya tree when at the same time she was in her father's laboratory. Then she realized that time must have passed, and she was lying on the ground, a grey blanket covering her.

The world went dark and when it was light again Dolly Hang's face had not gone away. Urgently, the child found herself trying to talk. She had never before felt such a blinding need to hack the words pellmell through the walls of her mouth and into the air, but the spell cast by the presence of Dolly Hang, and the blur of the Hang ancestors working their way around her locked the words away behind the root of her tongue, where they died, and in Dolly Hang's arms the child shivered and itched, and found that she could say nothing.

Her illness brought about a sudden change in Joachim's attitudes towards rearing the child. Now he became neurotically protective of the little mute, restricting her movements to a cruel and unnatural degree. The child, who had always taken her morning lessons out of doors, was now shut away inside the dark house. Lessons consisted entirely of reading in English. Although she was unable to speak or, apparently, to hear, Julia spent hours with books.

Joachim found that he was able to be at home more, and began to knuckle down at last to the composition of his monograph on the propagation of Pacific coral. Each morning he spent alone in his study, sifting through all the data he had tipped into a scatter of drawers through the years, and writing it all up carefully, in German, with his fountain pen, in a leatherbound ledger-sized journal he had purchased as a youth and had kept all these years for the purpose.

Each afternoon he took his daughter on nature excursions, although the routes he chose for her through the garden were always quite safe.

They made a strange sight in the Queensland sun,

the European 'doktor' with his neatly-trimmed goatee, his felt hat and walking stick, in his light cotton suit, and the small girl, her face grown into a mask of pale seriousness, with that quizzical look the deaf mute develops. She had no freckles now, not even a touch of the sun in her features, her long black hair tucked up under the brim of her sun hat, her delicately boned wrist cocked against the thought of any sudden attack from the bushes along the garden paths. Her eyes, flicking from side to side as she walked along the path had, as the summer passed, grown more and more disturbingly dark.

The child had a way of looking through her father which puzzled him. He did not read in it any rebuke for his actions. Behind that cool stare there was something taunting. Or as though she were inviting him to share a glimpse into the place where she continued to live.

During the season when it rained at the same hour every afternoon he often came upon her on the veranda on the southern, cooler side of the house, which he had filled with pots of his exotic plant specimens. One day she had her back to him and was apparently unaware of his approach, although Joachim was never entirely convinced of the genuineness of her affliction. The sound of the torrential rain drumming on the roof and in the trees was very loud.

Unseen by her, he spoke, describing all the wickedness he had in store for her, while the girl continued to stare ahead into the rain. When at last he walked around in front of Julia, for a long moment she seemed not to see him. These bouts of apathy he began to think of as her 'absences', in the mental notation of the scientist.

Although Joachim long worried that her brain had in some way been *affected*, the girl continued to display in her reading an undoubted intelligence. But as her twelfth birthday drew near and she began to menstruate, her grasp of the mathematical diminished to his profound disgust. She had no interest in staying up late into the night with her father in his wooden observatory in the garden, with his telescope and his charts, plotting the path of an approaching comet against the stars. This was of course Halley's Comet, as its orbit approached that of the earth in 1910. Now the girl's only interest was in romantic literature, and she did not stop at the cheap romantic novelettes she borrowed from her ill-educated governesses. She devoured all of Shakespeare in a matter of weeks, then memorized entire slabs from Palgrave's *Golden Treasury*. She read over and over obsessively that poem in which Coleridge describes how he approached the palace of Kubla Khan and heard the music played by the damsel with the dulcimer. All of this Joachim dismissed as contemptible, although as a scientist as well as a German he had to admit a grudging admiration for the works of Shakespeare.

The man went to extraordinary lengths so that his daughter might have European governesses. Invariably these young women wasted their train journeys north. Once he received a letter in reply to his advertisements in the coastal weekly newspaper from a widowed lady who happened to have a twelve year old daughter of her own. He thought that the companionship might have jolted Julia from her torpor. The other child, a spiteful, tow-headed Dutch girl, whose experience in the mission school on the coast had equipped her with a malice and cunning which far outmatched Julia's, was always favoured in disputes by the mother. Joachim could not bear to see the look of uncomprehending misery on his daughter's face, and he sent the woman away, although she was in all other respects a good and careful worker. But he sent her away not before he had taken her one night when she expected it least into his wooden observatory and seduced her in full view of Halley's comet.

In the classified columns of the *Mem Courier* his search for a governess continued. If only Joachim would have admitted it, his search was impossible because he was not looking for a governess so much as a successor in his bed to Julia's English mother. And only a woman who resisted his advances out in the wooden observatory would be worthy of this honour.

He thought he might have found such a lady when the Scottish-born Vera came up to live at the house at Duck River. Her nationality was close enough to English in his eyes to substitute for his darling dead Elizabeth. She was invited out into the observatory one night soon after she had arrived.

As she bent forward over the eyepiece of the telescope he ran his hand up her cool leg. She began screaming with such intensity that it required the administration of so much laudanum as to render her insensible. It was as she lay drugged that night that the scientist finally conquered her. When she awoke and deduced from the bloodstained sheets and from the extreme tenderness of her private parts what had occurred, she went away. Nevertheless, Joachim remembered her fondly afterwards as that *rara avis*, the genuinely virtuous woman.

Julia was thirteen and had begun to grow breasts. She was as isolated from her father as ever, almost as inaccessible, he told himself, as the mountains at the source of the Duck River he had once explored. Even with his scientific zeal, he found that he could not chart his daughter's 'northern reaches'.

His daughter's skin, now that she avoided the sun so completely, had begun to take on the same appearance as his wife's during her long period as an invalid: pale, anemic, the 'English complexion'. And one day at luncheon while they were eating soup he noticed that the shape of her teeth was changing. Her eye-teeth were developing in such a way that when she opened her mouth for food and closed it again the tips of her eye-teeth rested on her lower lip—just like his wife's, when she had been young. He felt the involuntary shower of memories rain through his mind.

On their infrequent visits to the coast he treated his daughter in public as though she were already his wife. He took her to the shops of the little port town dressed in her mother's clothes he had bought in Europe twenty years before. Her mother had been a tiny woman, but even so Julia had to lift the hems of the long dresses as she tripped along the hot main street under the verandas. They were beautiful clothes. She wore a tailored dress with tight-fitting sleeves and a short-backed jacket trimmed with velvet, embroidery and braid. There was another dress of lace-edged lilac chiffon she loved to wear, with a jewelled buckle on the velvet belt. Her father allowed her to wear to town her mother's little hat trimmed with an ostrich feather and a mauve veil which fell to just below her eyes.

With her grown-up dresses and extravagant hat he took her to the town's sad tea room, the Astoria, gloomy behind its wide veranda, next to a draper's. The draper, a short man in a grey apron, always scurried up to the door of his shop to watch them pass. There they sat up to tea and cakes in the window before taking the narrow-gauge train home in the late afternoon. Glimpsed through the window of the tea shop, or in the carriage of the train, the effect of the cosmetics and haberdashery was convincing, although when you looked more closely her painted little face was grotesque.

At home he supervised the undressing so that the costumes were properly stored where they had lived all these years in her mother's cedar wardrobe. One evening when they had driven the horse and trap home from the station and she had taken off the precious petticoats, he suddenly grasped her around the waist from behind. His fingers bit through her cotton shift and she turned around, fearing she had displeased him in some way. She was surprised when he was smiling through his beard.

He went to his study and came back with a leather-bound folio from which he took several watercolour paintings he had made of various species of birds. On some of the thick pieces of cartridge paper he had replicated exactly the stuffed birds on his study wall; on others he had sketched birds mating.

It excited him when he came across a pair of birds

53

hurling and fluttering against each other in such a way in the garden. He had often taken up his stick to point this phenomenon out to her. He even indulged himself in preening little pirouettes in imitation of the birds, and laughed and bade her join in the game.

Now, beside the cedar wardrobe, the games continued.

In those intervals between governesses and when Julia stayed shut up with her books, Joachim had become casual in the matter of nudity around the house. He had dismissed all the servants the previous year out of deference to his ideas on racial contamination.

In the late afternoons when customarily he bathed, and the slanting light fell deep through the slats of the shutters and along the passages, there seemed to be a third presence, quite apart from the man and the girl, and which could not entirely be ascribed to the memory of the brooding, ill woman who had died in the room at the back of the house, and to whom all the months of enemas and foments had given the appearance of utter lifelessness long before it was actually so. Now, in the afternoons, there was something subtly and inevitably manipulative in the silences.

On the occasions when he did have a woman from the brothel at Mem make the journey up to the Duck River, Joachim was not always careful to ensure that the bedroom door was completely closed. By this time he had his doubts about the authenticity of his daughter's deafness and on one occasion that summer, the woman's howls of slaked lust brought the girl silently to put her eye to the crack of the door. Joachim noticed the slight disturbance in the configuration of light there (in spite of the fact that at that moment he was still in complete possession of the woman) and he knew that it was with jealousy and not shame that the girl slunk away, her childhood finally behind her.

It was the rainy season again, the season when Joachim, who hated the wind, spent entire days in bed with the shutters closed, locked into a semi-permanent artificial night. He sat up in his bed with his spectacles on, the candles burning, his writing tray balanced on his large stomach. Reference books he had carried in from his study weeks before were stacked up on the floor as high as the bed, his notes and manuscripts scattered around him.

During these times, Julia's household duties doubled, then trebled, so that whenever she had a moment to herself she fell asleep. She had to cook for him, and in spite of his inactivity his appetite was voracious. She had regularly to empty his chamberpots, of which there were two, one for each bodily function. And she massaged his paunch to ease his pain through his attacks of flatulence. Then, as though it were a natural concomitant of her nursing duties, with his wind expelled and his member erect, she made of her mouth a repository for his semen.

The longer his periods of hibernation, the less inclined he was to leave his bed at all. As with his other corporeal urges, there had been another subtle transformation in the relationship between them. Their sex, since she had begun menstruating, had retained the spontaneity of that first time they had begun 'playing birds', the game by which he had introduced her to partial penetration. She accepted it as quite natural for him to take her at any moment of the day or night. In the kitchen while she was at her chores, outside in the garden, even at table during a half-finished meal, Joachim would simply move behind her, raise her skirts and take her with several brutal efficient strokes. This was always his method of enjoying her, as if to have to look at that pale bewildered face while he was performing his act would have been too much for even his hardened heart to bear. From this early age of thirteen she had come to accept the insertion of his erect penis as a natural and unremarkable bodily function.

Now, as her father spent longer and longer in bed, she learned to judge his sexual needs by the clock. These duties became so mundane that she performed them without thinking. After she had helped him break his wind, she pulled her long black hair from her face and rested her cheek on the soft paunch and performed her perfunctory but efficient act of fellation. From that position she found she could stretch her neck over the edge of the bed and spit out his semen into one of the china chamberpots.

Sometimes, resting face down over the side of the bed like this, listening to the slowing rasp of his breathing and the monsoon winds outside shaking the trees and rattling the iron roof, she looked at his manuscript scattered across the floor, the pages criss-crossed with his spidery German hand in black ink. Half closing her eyes, the lines rearranged themselves in new patterns and she liked to speculate from these upon their possible meaning. Gradually, from recognizing a word here and another there, she began to decipher lines of his text. Also, there were his beautiful drawings of plant specimens, rock formations, birds, animals, and the vast cities of coral building themselves under the water. She loved to look at the delicate night blues, the Venetian reds, magentas, russets and cyclamens; at the rose, dragon's blood and cinnibar; at the sea greens and jades and viridians of the coral which he had captured in his water colours. And forever after that when she heard German spoken or saw it printed on a page she was back in the dark airless atmosphere of that room with the taste of semen in her mouth.

It was during one of these extended periods in bed that Joachim developed a skin disease. A patch of leathery skin had appeared then spread ominously from its original site under the pit of his left arm, across his plump and pendulous breast and had begun its slow creep down his belly.

At first the scaly skin had contracted into what looked like fungus spores. Then it had yellowed, then browned, and the patch of skin had toughened so that it resembled a piece of cow's hide. If Joachim himself was worried about his skin disease he did not reveal it to the girl.

Sometimes Julia believed that her father was actually becoming a mushroom. The tough skin on his stomach changed colours with the tides of the moon. The hide on his belly grew a rich deep brown, but at certain times of the month she awoke in the night to find his patch an iridescent orange, or a pale yellow speckled with brown spots. In the mornings, if he were well enough to occupy himself with his manuscript, she surreptitiously looked at the fungi on the walls to find that they too had changed colour. In this way Joachim's disease and the damp growth on the walls of the house kept secret tabs on each other.

With each wet season, the house had fallen deeper into decay. Mosses crept around the window frames, tree ferns sprouted from the outside walls, and when leaves and overhanging branches fell onto the roof they rotted there and provided a rich compost base for the next generation of parasitical growth. A small softwood tree with shiny oval-shaped leaves grew out of the veranda and the roots hung down through the holes in the rusted iron roof, where they tickled the face of anyone foolish enough to walk along that veranda in the dark. It was from one of these twisted clumps of roots one afternoon as Julia sat alone in an old wicker chair reading her *Golden Treasury* and listening to the groans of her father and a woman making love inside the darkened house, that a green tree snake began to unwind itself.

Every muscle in her body taut, she waited for the snake to fade naturally out of existence and become an innocent strand of tree root again. She watched its sharp eye, its calm reptilian mouth as the green snake arched its back and swayed even lower through the air towards her.

Hours later, when her father finally found her, she looked more dead than alive. Joachim's difficulty was that the floorboards around the hole where she had fallen were so badly decayed that when he knelt to stretch his arms down to the filthy bundle that was his daughter, his own knee went through the wood and he was just able to save himself from falling down into the pit beneath the veranda. He was calling her name all the time, over and over, then swearing in German, and it was these cries which brought the whore out from the dark innards of the house, still wrapping a red housecoat around her body.

Joachim fetched an iron crow bar from the shed and plied away the rotten floorboards until there was space for him to lower himself. Woodlice jumped in the gloom. There were unnamed and unnameable insects, strange hybrid and mutated millipedes and leeches already making themselves at home in her mouth and nostrils and ears. Joachim did not dare to look beneath her torn clothing for fear of the life forms he might find there.

Once he had carried the girl into the house, nothing could revive her, neither sal volatile, nor the application of hot and cold flannels to her forehead. Ice to the temples and vigorous slapping of the face all failed to bring back any sign of consciousness in her.

Joachim and the woman from the town watched over Julia all night. By the next morning the girl had 'turned the corner'. In the dawn Julia continued to breathe and Joachim was relieved that he would not, after all, have to make the twelve mile journey to the little coastal town where Dr Perkins had his practice. In the course of the night he had learned from the woman that Julia was with child.

Julia's fear of snakes extended to such a point that she refused to touch even the most trivial and harmless object. It was too much to ask that she pick up a rubber mat for fear of the cold-bloodedness of the material. Sometimes a lady's glove on the hallstand suddenly filled with energy and moved for her. The desiccated texture of string or rope induced fits of shaking and vomiting. Even the red silken cord which fastened her father's dressing gown had to be hidden away in a drawer because of its cool liquid slithery quality and because, in a certain angle of light, it appeared to Julia to be moving.

She often sat with her back to the slender coils in the big jars of methylated spirits in her father's abandoned laboratory. In the big room the paint was flaking from the walls and every surface was covered with a thick layer of dust. Still, she used to steal in there sometimes, when she knew her father would not surprise her, and when she could safely take the key from the pocket of his waistcoat hanging over the bedroom chair, and sit in the dim air with all those smells of science.

The woman whose howls of love had disturbed Julia's sleep that distant afternoon and brought her to put her eye to the door was a real Italian prostitute named Tina Terrina. After that first visit she had regularly taken the train north from Mem to stay for several days at a time with the unfortunate 'professori' at Duck River, for a financial consideration, of course.

That first afternoon had pleased the girl. She had thought her father was hurting the interloper and that soon he would send her away on the Sunday train. But on another level, Tina Terrina fascinated her. She painted her mouth in a big red heart, and her brown arms hanging bare from her blouse were golden-bangled.

Tina Terrina never seemed comfortable in a dress, when she wore one. She was always looking down at the bosom and trying to pick off an imaginary piece of fluff.

In the later afternoons, after the dark airless hours of lovemaking with the rotten-skinned man, they took the girl down to the river to bathe. On the first such afternoon Julia saw that Tina Terrina was without bathing costume. She simply ran from the buggy through the gum trees to the edge of that vast plain of green water that was the Duck River and began taking off her clothes. Julia watched as the woman undressed and she saw the plump brown nipples, the dimpled thighs, the great white buttocks which hung down in folds of fat, the shocking expanse of her black pubic hair. Tina Terrina unfastened the long braid which hung down her back and pushed herself off into the river, causing scarcely a ripple in the thick green scum on the surface. Then the girl watched her father undress, baring that unsightly skin, and follow the woman in.

Julia sat on the river bank in her ballooning cotton frock and watched the two figures at sport in the water. Her face still wore the slightly puzzled expression of the mute. How could she compete with such ripeness of flesh? She, with her smooth dark nipples, the little mound of her stomach growing so slowly? She was astounded by the woman's vulgar maternal beauty. Even Julia felt that she wanted to nuzzle her face into Tina's slack belly, to push her mouth towards those big soft breasts.

Tina Terrina's visits became more frequent, and increasingly she took up Joachim's time. He no longer spent all day in bed. His monograph had been abandoned during his illness and returning health did not rekindle his interest in it. He looked forward to the relief of Tina's visits, to the drive in the buggy to the railway station to see her running along the platform in her lurid clothes, changing her cardboard suitcase from hand to hand as she ran.

She would arrive at the station from Mem in her gaudy dresses and hats, but in the succeeding days her dress would diminish gradually until she was getting around the house in a pair of silk drawers, her great tawny breasts jouncing as she moved. Some afternoons after their long lovemaking she walked around the house in nothing at all.

There was something else, a kind of redemption: Tina Terrina had casually unearthed in Joachim the pleasure of giving. One time, as she was leaving from the station, he had pushed the roll of tattered pound notes into her hand. She had counted them by habit, then, acting on impulse, stuffed them back into Joachim's paws in such a resolute way that he offered no argument. There was a glow of gratitude on the man's face and the moment stayed with him for a long time.

After one of her visits he had found her gold crucifix on its chain amongst the sheets and bedclothes. He had worn it himself, the weight of the gold brushing the diseased skin of his chest, intending to return it to her on her next visit. She asked him to keep it as a gift, and he never took it off again. He became devoted to Tina Terrina and each time the sexual act was repeated between them that moment of gratitude was reinforced. That moment on the station contained ingredients for

Joachim which might have made a second marriage, had it not made instead a kind of religious conversion. One day, when he was staying overnight at the brothel at Mem, he accompanied Tina to the Catholic church, confessed his sins to the womanly Irish priest and thereafter called himself a Catholic.

Julia panicked at the prospect of sharing her father, although now he was careful to avoid physical contact with her. There were secrets to be kept from any intruder and it unsettled her when, from her vantage at the gap in the door, she saw Joachim initiate Tina Terrina into some of them.

She added her own distinctive smell to the mouldering house so that for days after her visits Julia would catch herself thinking that Tina Terrina was still there. No amount of opening windows could douse those fruity odours the woman had left. Nor could the sweetmeats, which Tina Terrina brought with her by the bagful from the store in Mem, and which she would grudgingly dole out one at a time to Julia in return for some service, disguise her putrid breath.

Julia found her one afternoon in Joachim's bedroom staring at the books which had been left months before in a scatter across the floor. She puzzled over the weird script and exclaimed at the beauty of his sketches and his watercolours of the coral. Julia went in and sat beside her and entered again the world of coral she had inhabited as a child. Another afternoon Julia found her in front of the mirror in Joachim's bedroom rubbing scented oil into her body to disguise her smell as much as to soothe her skin which had grown brown and scaly so that at times it looked as though it was covered with cobwebs. It was only later, when Tina Terrina began to exude the same yeasty smell as her father, did the girl realize Tina Terrina had contracted Joachim's skin disease.

One night when her father was away with Tina in Mem, Julia sat alone on the veranda with the moths beating around her face. So big and white were these moths, they were like blind graceless birds blown in from the ocean, and Julia was suddenly seized by the premonition that Joachim would not return. The wind began to move through the gum trees.

She began to cry, a dry grizzling in her ears which seemed to come from outside herself, from the garden somewhere. 'Papa,' it cried. The moths sensed her fear and redoubled their attack. Julia had never minded moths before, but now the more the panic rose up in her the faster the moths whirred around the kerosene lamp and flapped against her face. She caught one in anger, cupping it in her hands, and carefully tore the wings off its husk-dry body. The other moths homed in on the lamp, and it was several minutes before it occurred to her to douse the wick. The creatures fell away and Julia was left alone while the night noises multiplied in the darkness and she began to cry again, simply and forcefully, like any child. 'Papa, Papa!' she cried. Miraculously, the words were forming once more in her mouth. For the rest of her life whenever she cried she would always feel the cottony wings of the moths between her fingers.

Storms were common at this time of the year. There would be a strange quality in the light and a perfect stillness when all the birds disappeared. Men would huddle on the docks securing the fishing boats and looking nervously out to sea, waiting for the palm trees on Charlotte Island to begin to bend.

But this storm had blown in during the night. Joachim looked out the windows of the Hotel Continental through the driving rain to see the muddy river flowing through the street. The sound of rain hammering on the iron roof was so loud he had to lean across and shout into Tina Terrina's ear to make himself heard.

As the floodwaters rose during the next morning, the occupants of the hotel had to climb the stairs to the second storey where they held on to the rails of the balcony. They yelled out to the men in the boats down in the street to let them know they were safe. It was then, to Joachim's profound amazement, that he saw his daughter race by in the wooden skiff he had kept moored to the little jetty in the Duck River all these years.

A flock of small parrots flitted across the surface of the dark water, just above Julia's head. She threw her hands up to her face. The birds, bright crimson and green and blue, sped off through the eucalypts in the rain.

The river grasses along the banks were already submerged by the rising water. The rain increased its tempo and blinded her and now the boat could do nothing but race with the current, bumping against bobbing timbers and the carcases of animals.

She lay on her back with the sound of the rushing water and the straining timbers of the old boat so constant it might have been her own breathing. Ahead, the river raced into darkness through the tunnel of the wind. Then the boat was hurled at the walls of solid water and twice she felt it somersault.

The broken tops of trees protruded through the water's surface and, as the wind dropped and the sun came out for a moment, Julia found herself in a green cave of light. She saw the wet grey wood of a fallen tree trunk suddenly very close to her cheek, felt the hollow knock against the bone of her head, and the light vanished. There were invisible fingers on her legs just below the surface of the water. She slowed, then stopped, while debris continued to race past her. Reeds slashed at her and the fishing net that had wrapped itself around her tightened.

Time passed and sounds came to Julia from the world. A dog barked. A toad was swelling on the edge of her vision. Julia screwed up her eyes tightly, waiting for the creature to fade, but when she opened them there was a man's face very close to her own. He had no beard and his hair was whiter than oats. He had blue eyes with pale lashes and wore a sleeveless black vest with a round white collar. And the bottom part of his body was rubbery, shiny, like a fish. Then he did something which terrified her: he opened his mouth and laughter rang out.

An extraordinary crime occurred. King Edward was up on the wall watching Julia in the stationmaster's office at Mem. She was lying on a camp stretcher in the corner, her hand on her swollen belly. And there, above her on the wall the man with the beard like her father's was watching her. Would the King unhook himself from the wall and walk across to her, smiling and bearded in his uniform, wearing his sword and his royal blue sash and, not taking his blue eyes from hers, undress her? But it was the stationmaster who was fumbling out of his clothes, leaving his long woollen undershirt hanging down around the tops of his legs. His face was flushed with the effort of getting his shoes off, and his three days' growth of whiskers gave him an evil mien. He reached beneath her and she felt his fingernails bite into her buttocks. When he had finished he got up from the truckle bed and turned towards the wall where the portrait of the King hung and laughed. Then he buttoned his trousers firmly.

Gradually the smell of boiling chicken filled the room and Julia realized she was starving. With a grey blanket wrapped around her, she went across and quietly opened the door. The man dressed as a preacher had his black-coated back to her, stirring a pot on the woodstove. He surprised her by speaking without looking around. 'I've been wondering when you'd be coming in.'

When at last he turned his face to her she was shocked by its kindness. The preacher appeared to be unperturbed by her staring. He clumsily put his pipe in the corner of his wet mouth and said, 'Me and my fishing. It's a passion with me. I put in the nets before the storm.' He looked around the dismal little kitchen for a match, then turned suddenly back to her, smiling. 'My dear,' he said. 'God told me he was sending me a wife.'

As was his habit on festive occasions, Willy Paradise arranged a fireworks display in the garden. He was determined that this year on Julia's birthday, in spite of her illness, the fireworks would be more spectacular than ever before. Hoy T'Hoy, who was a traditional fireworks maker from the village and who always planned and executed the pyrotechnics in village festivals, was in charge. Early that morning Mr Hoy had secured his skyrockets to a row of sharpened bamboo stakes along one flank of the mission's rose garden. On boards nailed to the veranda rails he had fixed his Roman torches and Catherine wheels, while at designated places around the ground he had concealed small charges called 'tom-toms', whose dull thuds would send clods of earth showering skywards. He had also laid out on the veranda assorted fireworks which were to be thrown by hand: firecrackers of various sizes and force, fizgigs, torches and sparklers in every imaginable colour,

as well as the fireworks unique to this particular craftsman, and to which the villagers had given names like
comets, suns, moons and stars. The crackers, stacked by
their hundreds, had been painstakingly handrolled over
months, carefully packed with saltpetre, and covered
with shiny red paper, red being the Chinese colour for
celebration. Hoy T'Hoy had built his rockets, shells and
Roman candles with his own hallmark of 'stars' which
filled the sky with coloured fires as the rockets burst.
He had prepared the customary white fire, the gerbes
and fountains made of potassium chlorate, as well as
the magnesium-brilliant, strontium-red, barium-green,
sodium-yellow and copper-blue.

In the garden, where it would be clearly visible from
the veranda, Mr Hoy had spent the afternoon construct-
ing the main set piece of the display, which had been
designed by Willy Paradise himself. On the edges there
would be waterfalls of fire and 'tree-pieces', trunks and
branches of fire which shot up and remained in the
night sky. In the middle, in the position of honour, Mr
Hoy had built the framework of wood onto which he
had secured the fireworks which would become wheels
moving in the vertical and horizontal planes. And there,
constructed in bamboo on the wooden lattice framework,
the Paradise surprise would reveal itself: the design of
the Union Jack picked out in lances of colour.

When Ayres arrived at the local station on the two
o'clock train from Shanghai, Julia was waiting in the
little green motor-car to pick him up. Ayres immediately
wondered who had been behind the invitation to cele-
brate her thirty-first birthday. The invitation had arrived

in the minister's hand, a short and formal note outlining the evening's proposed activities, and Ayres had replied with an equal formality.

Julia had just returned to the mission after spending a week at Hangchow. She had been staying in an English-run hotel overlooking one of the lakes there in the care of another missionary lady, one Gerthilde Platz. Ayres, of course, knew all about this. Julia herself had approached him on the subject a fortnight before, while dressing herself at the conclusion of their regular Tuesday afternoon. Willy's consent to her travelling to Hangchow, she had said, depended on Ayres' agreement that the trip would not be harmful to her and that it would not in any way interfere with the programme of treatment Ayres had laid out for her and which seemed to be succeeding so well. Ayres had seen that the trip meant a great deal to her.

Hangchow was 118 miles away by train, a place of lovely lake scenery at the foot of the Eye of Heaven mountains. The proverb has it: 'There is heaven above and Hangchow below.' Ayres believed the change of air might have done Julia some good and lifted her spirits. The greatest danger in her going was that any undue excitement might overstimulate her frail nervous system and precipitate another manic swerve into hysterical breakdown, far from family and friends. If she were to miss one of her regular unburdenings of her psyche to Ayres, her hallucinations might build up in her mind. Nevertheless, he had given his permission in a note to Willy on the condition that she took a first-class compartment, that she stayed in a good hotel, that her German missionary friend ensured that she avoided all excitement, and that she continued to take only regular five grains of morphine by injection upon retiring. All this was promised and Julia had left for her holiday. On the Thursday Ayres had received a picture postcard of the West Lake captioned on the back in her usual violent hand: 'Dear Doctor, Greetings from the land of the lakes. Wonderful, radiant! And surprise! I am completely cured of animal pains here! Julia Paradise.' Now, two days later, here she was sitting at the wheel of her husband's motor car.

Ayres and Julia drove along the dirt road from the station. It was potholed and rutted; they could travel only slowly. They passed through a region of little farming villages. The countryside was spectacularly lush, the entire river plain a green carpet of crop and vegetation.

Julia sat calmly at the wheel of Willy's little car. She seemed less tense, but was relaxed in an unnatural and uncharacteristic way that was not entirely convincing. He thought that perhaps she was merely trying to impress him with the effects of her holiday. The strain on her face, always present in the city, had vanished. There were smiles. There was even, in response to a passing comment of Ayres, laughter. For Ayres there was a sense of unreality about being together out of doors, away from his dark room and bed, and the long airless hours of Julia talking.

He ran a finger down her shoulder blade, fine as a child's. All the time there was the river in the distance.

They crossed countless small wooden bridges only wide enough for one cart and so low and near the surface of the water that he heard above the noise of the motor car the rush of the filling canals.

After they had been travelling for half an hour, Julia suddenly pulled up. They were at a bend in the river where the valley had narrowed and huge white boulders stood around in the sun. A pebble bank sloped steeply to the murky tidal water. She reached to open the door, then slipped out of the car and began half-walking, half-sliding down the steep pebble bank. Ayres followed her, the small rocks spilling away from under his boots.

About two hundred yards away there was a small group of people at work on the rocks. Some of them were fishing with long bamboo poles while others had waded out into the water, setting their nets. Although from that distance Ayres could not see the actual nets, they were close enough for him to see what they were doing.

Ayres and Julia stood for a long time watching the fishermen and the expanse of water before them. She said, 'You know, there are things here I can look at and look at. I keep seeing beauty here I never thought possible. I come from such an ugly country.' She broke off and stared down at her shoes furiously, apparently impatient at the effort it took to force her thoughts into words. Then she changed again, and went on in a bright cheery voice. 'You see that man over there with the fishermen—on that first rock there? With the hat? That's Willy.' Ayres said he was surprised.

'He comes down here on Saturdays to fish with them. Those other men are our houseboys and gardeners. He comes every Saturday, without fail. He gives them all a half-holiday, as though they were Englishmen . . .' Her eyes were blazing.

'He's paying cook double to work this afternoon. The

houseboys tonight will want the same. Willy panders them. Crawls on his hands and knees to meet with their approval—like some insect. How they must be laughing at him! He treats them—I don't know—as if they are our equals. Worse. I think he's trying to be like them!'

Ayres said, 'Your place must not be far from here.'

She fumbled in the pocket of the cardigan she wore and took out a packet of English Players, lighted one and said, 'No. Not far at all.' She continued to look at the river, then went on more calmly, 'He often doesn't come home until after dinner. He eats rice with their families in the village.'

'Do none of them live in the mission?'

She laughed at that. 'Some soldiers came here last week while I was in Hangchow. Scared them all off. Now the girls have had to go home, too. Bloody Kuomintang soldiers sleep in the schoolhouse now.'

'Why does your husband not complain? He must have contacts. I myself know the first secretary at the Embassy.'

'Willy says we are here to earn the people's love. Not command it. You should hear him. You'd think he was a member of the Kuomintang himself.' Her face had changed completely during this outburst. A look of utter misery had come over her. She was raw-eyed, her lips thin and drawn back from her teeth in a kind of contemptuous smile and her hand with the cigarette shook. She said, just as bitterly as before, 'I've never known a man to love the Chinese as he does. Poor Willy. He so believes in what he's doing.'

Ayres looked again at the distant figure, indistinguishable from the other figures around him. The sun was on the surface of the river. There was a peacefulness about the scene that was unimaginable twenty miles away in the city with its strikes, the sudden changes of mood on the Bund when the head of a march appeared at the end of the street. You heard the noise before you saw them, then slowly the Bund filled up with thousands upon thousands of Chinese strikers. The shootings, the grisly discoveries in the dawn of men hanging from lamp-posts, the days of uneasy truce when it seemed the strike might be broken, then the British and American gunboats anchored in the Soochow Creek, from the armadas cruising up and down the Yangtze—all that seemed very much further away than twenty miles just then, that moment of sunlight on the water, that Saturday afternoon when Ayres was on his way to the little mission school for girls.

From the outside, the mission seemed a happy, sunny spot for the girls of middle-class Chinese families to spend their youth; not at all like the dreary dungeon of a public school in Edinburgh where Ayres, as a fat boy, had been miserable. Ayres did not see any of the soldiers: they only returned here to sleep at night. This little mission school with its timber and stucco buildings, its bungalows dotted amongst the vast well-tended gardens, its stands of trees and roses laid out neatly in rows was more English than Ayres' school had been and, walking in the rose garden with Willy, it again occurred to Ayres that he seemed to be a world away from strikes and marches in Shanghai. More than anything, it seemed too peaceful, too idyllic a place to billet the officers of a platoon of the Kuomintang army in the final stage of its advance upon Shanghai.

Willy Paradise's study looked more like the preparation room in a museum of the natural sciences than the place where a missionary clergyman might write his Sunday sermons. Three walls were lined with the scientific texts he had brought on the ship with him from Australia. In the centre of the room was the large deal table on which he had laid out the paraphernalia of his scientific researches.

The Reverend Willy Paradise was happy to show the physician, who was at least nominally his brother in science, his prized German microscope, his trays of neatly labelled butterfly and insect specimens, as well as his great leather-bound folios of birds, each painstakingly reproduced in watercolour on the expensive handmade paper he bought from a craftsman in the city.

He showed Ayres the drawers full of his local rock samples, and the ragged beginnings of the manuscript which he hoped later to publish privately at home in retirement—a fine, weighty monograph on the formation of Pacific coral reefs.

Ayres was determined to ask the man some of the questions which had over the weeks insinuated themselves in his mind like Julia's snakes. He began by asking Willy where he and Julia had first met. The question seemed to take the reverend gentleman by surprise. He smiled, hesitated, and lifted the wet stem of his pipe to his lips. 'As a matter of fact, it was at a dance in Brisbane,' he said. 'By the way, I trust we may judge her little holiday a success. She certainly looks all the brighter for it.'

'Apparently.'

'My word she does . . .' His words trailed off and he took his pipe out of his mouth and examined it. Then he looked quietly back at his guest with his pale blue eyes. 'I must say, Ayres, I chose an inauspicious time for a celebration. When all this is happening. How long will it last, do you think?'

'You'd know better than I.'

'But the strike, Ayres. The struggle of the people. You're on the spot. What do they say at your club?'

'What they always say, I suppose. The usual mixture of doomsayers and sabre-rattlers. You have heard, have you not, that the Consul is recalling all missionaries who are British subjects from the inland?'

'I've heard it.'

'Apparently some of them are refusing to come into the Ports.'

'We are close enough to Shanghai not to worry too much.'

'Yes, but those others. I wouldn't give twopence for their chances. It will be the Boxers all over again. That's what they're saying at the club. Although of course I take little interest in the wretched politics of the matter.'

'Of course.'

They sat in silence for a few minutes, then Ayres spoke:

'This German lady who went to Hangchow with your wife. Is she a teaching missionary here as well?'

'Miss Platz? Why, yes.'

'You haven't noticed, have you, when they're alone together, whether they talk in German or in English?'

'In English, of course. Miss Platz speaks better English than you or I, if the truth were known. She was educated in England. At the Somerville College at Oxford.'

'Yes, but I mean—Julia's father was a German, wasn't he?'

'But she can't speak German! Her mother was English. That's the language we speak in Australia! You can't take any notice of her ravings when she's ill.'

'I'd like to ask you a question entirely related to her illness. Your answer may help in her full recovery. Yet, it is a personal question and one which you may choose not to answer.' Ayres too had been filling his pipe. Now lighting it, and sucking the heavy sweet-scented tobacco down into his lungs, he felt his heart beating quickly. He went on straight away, to get his question out into the open. 'When you married, was your wife a virgin?'

Willy Paradise looked away. He let his eye rove over the glass trays of insects, the dry husks of their thoraxes pinned to the mounting boards; then up to the fourth wall of the room, which bore a variety of bright stuffed birds: toucans, parakeets, rainbow birds, larks, tits, chats and honeyeaters of the white-naped and striped species. He continued to stare at the birds for some moments, as if he had not heard correctly and they might help him. Finally he said, 'The Methodist Church, unlike the Church of England and the Church of Rome, does not insist on consummation.'

'I'm sorry. I don't quite see—'

'She's a virgin, Ayres. She was and she still is. We've

never *been* together in our marriage. Not once.' Willy Paradise took the pipe out of his mouth and blinked back at Ayres with dignity.

Ayres said, 'Tell me about her father. You did meet him?'

'I knew him well.'

'What kind of a man was he?'

'A man of entirely impeccable character.'

'Is he still alive?'

'As far as I am aware. Longevity runs in the Kohl family.'

'Kohl, did you say?'

'Julia's family name. Her father's name is Johannes Kohl.'

'Not Joachim?'

'Of course not. Who is Joachim?'

'He is a farmer? In North Queensland? But at the same time he is—what shall I call him—a man of science?'

'A man of science! No. Well, in a manner of speaking he is a man of science. He's a dentist, Ayres. You mustn't mind if I seem puzzled by all these questions.'

Ayres ignored him and went on, as though irrelevantly, 'Can you tell me where I might find the Duck River in Australia?'

'I am afraid I can't. If it exists it must be very small indeed. I don't mind telling you that I pride myself on being a keen student of the geography of my native land.'

'Nor have you ever heard of a coastal town called Mem? Am I correct in that?'

'Quite correct.' Willy Paradise nodded equably. 'But

perhaps you had better explain what you mean by asking all these questions.'

Ayres shrugged. He suddenly felt very tired indeed.
There was only one more question to ask. He opened
his mouth and heard his own disembodied voice. 'Mr
Paradise, have you any interest in astronomy?'

The clergyman seemed relieved by the question. He
beamed at him and his pink forehead shone. 'Why yes.
But how did you know? My wife must have mentioned
it to you. Actually we have built ourselves a fairly so-
phisticated little observatory in the garden at the back.
We encourage our students to take an interest in science.
It's only a six-inch telescope, but it's a comet seeker.
Comet seekers are always small; you need a large ratio
between the diameter of the lens and the focal length.
It's because comets are diffuse and have a low surface
brightness. It's a German telescope, though the equa-
torial mounting was made in America. Ah, many's the
night I've spent out there, sweeping the skies and check-
ing my charts. And I don't mind telling you that I've
had one or two notices of my sightings printed in the
scientific journals, both here and abroad. No Paradise's
Comet, though. Not yet, at any rate. One day, perhaps!
In fact, I'm rather inordinately proud of our little observatory. I'm looking forward to showing it to you.'

It was dusk and the moon had risen. Ayres stood at the
window of his room. From this vantage on the upper
storey he could see beyond the mission grounds to the
lush green valley, the canals, the tumbledown stone
buildings of a village and, in the distance, catching the
last red light of the afternoon sun, what looked like the

edge of a lake, but what was really the near shore of the river. Below him were English lawns, English trees, and a rose garden bordering the drive at the side, where a lone gardener was still at work. At the centre of the pattern of paths was a small stone fountain which had been partly reduced to rubble. The gardener moved along the rose bushes, stooping, pruning, cutting, sawing, and even from the distance between his window and the rose garden and even though the light had failed, Ayres could tell that the gardener was a woman. She was barefoot. She wore a pair of men's trousers and over them a hessian sack strapped on with a belt, like an apron; a vest; a collarless striped shirt with the sleeves rolled up over her biceps. He could see, now that she was below him, drawing water from the hand-pump at the well, the way her arms and shoulders made sinewy mounds of muscle. She carried the metal buckets of water back to where she had been working, pausing to splash this rosebush and that.

Ayres stood back and let the voile curtain fall. As he did so he caught his reflection in the mirror of the dressing table. His face was dark and his own expression was hidden from him. He walked over to his large suitcase which lay on top of the low chest of drawers, and from his medical bag next to it he took a small phial of vivid blue glass, which had been wrapped in a piece of cotton waste in one of the compartments. He uncorked it, lifted it to his nostrils as though it were a cologne to be sniffed, sipped from it, corked it again, returned it to the compartment, locked the bag and returned the key to his vest pocket. He sat on the side of the narrow bed and stared at the window. He thought of Julia Paradise and the net she had cast with such casual accuracy across his path: the hints planted, her silky narrative woven to confound him, an entire childhood left hanging in the air. Lying on the bed in his shirtsleeves, Ayres was a dream, Julia's story was a dream: just a different kind of opium-eating.

Later, when it was quite dark the four Europeans assembled on the veranda to watch the skyrockets.

People from the village kept respectfully to the borders of the lawns, although the more adventurous boys climbed the trees to improve their view.

At the first sound of the fireworks a group of soldiers wearing the drab green uniforms of the Kuomintang army came out of the schoolhouse at the back of the mission. They were capless and their uniforms were unbuttoned. They had been drinking rice wine and appeared dazed by the commotion which confronted them. Two went back inside to fetch their rifles, as though suspecting an artillery attack. When the soldiers had satisfied themselves it was all harmless enough, they joined in the spirit of the thing, whooping and laughing and firing several volleys in the air.

But when the Union Jack sprang into lights, hissing with its brilliantly coloured flares, their mood changed. There were shouts and angry gestures and two of them began methodically to smash their rifle butts through the windows of the schoolhouse. The Reverend Paradise looked for a moment as though he might go down and speak to them, but Julia grabbed his arm and held onto it tightly, and led them all inside.

The swooping sighs of the rockets could still be heard from the diningroom. It was a small room, nearly filled by the table and chairs, and a lamp cast a strong yellow light over their faces, so that everyone looked slightly ill. Ayres found himself seated opposite the woman he had observed earlier in the garden.

Miss Platz looked every inch the schoolteacher: a big woman in her dark and unfashionable clothes who kept her shoulders very erect. She had a patrician nose and her eyes shone with an absolute confidence in the way they saw things. Because of its plainness and luminosity, even her basin haircut, her face reminded him of Joan of Arc.

A soup tureen appeared, the boy vanished and Willy began to say Grace. Ayres bowed his head but did not close his eyes. He watched Julia at the head of the table in her shabby old cardigan. She had gone to no effort to dress for the occasion, wearing no rouge on her cheeks or lips, her hair uncombed and her face haggard and tired-looking. Willy wore his usual clerical collar and Ayres felt conspicuous in his dinner jacket and black tie. Through the meal Julia was perfectly agreeable, although tentative, uncertain. When her husband asked whether she had enjoyed the fireworks she smiled down at her hands and nodded her head quickly. There was a strained excitement in her and when she turned her head Ayres saw that the tendons in her throat stood out.

Willy helped her tear the wrapping paper from Ayres' Morocco album for her photographs; then from his own gift, a handsome edition of Coleridge. She flicked through the slim volume until she had found the page she wanted, then snapped it shut, as though afraid to let her pleasure show. Miss Platz alone had apparently failed to provide a gift.

Ayres rarely spoke. He muttered a word or two in reply to a question; a 'Hmm' or 'Mmm', encouraging Willy to go on. Ayres seemed the most relaxed of them all, elbow on the table, shirt cuff showing, a bearded cheek resting in the palm of his hand. When Willy or Miss Platz spoke, his eyes stayed on them, bobbing his head to show he followed. He watched as Julia became more restless. Her tic resumed. Occasionally she sucked back her saliva or sniffed loudly. She ate little, and lighted a Players before the others had finished eating.

The pudding was produced, and Ayres, who had a sweet tooth, took particular interest. It was a rich wine trifle—an aberration for Methodists, Ayres thought. There was no wine served at table. The fat layers of yellow custard alternated with sponge cake, soaked fruit with almonds and whipped cream, the whole floating in a sauce of port wine and another syrup, a clear caramel liquor, traceable to no particular ingredient and which formed itself (by alchemy, for all Ayres knew) in the best trifles. It was excellent and Ayres was pleased to be helped to a second serving. A cake was brought in with thirty-one candles blazing. After the birthday song, Willy proposed a toast to the King in sparkling ginger ale. His butter knife rang against the side of his crystal glass, and three of them rose. Miss Platz remained stubbornly seated. 'Surely we can afford to be just a little patriotic?' Willy chided her good-naturedly.

'I know where patriotism leads,' she said. She spoke in an Oxford drawl which, with her slight German accent, never quite avoided sounding disdainful.

After the toast, in the absence of either brandy or port, Julia and Miss Platz sat on, and Ayres offered Willy a cigar.

Willy waggled his finger at Miss Platz. 'But you're a patriot yourself, my dear. You opposed your country-men in the war.' His manner was teasing and indulgent, and his gestures with the big Havana added to his gran-diloquent air. Ayres liked the man a lot less as a host than as a victim.

'I opposed the war,' she pointed out quietly. 'If Christ were really present in our hearts he would make of us all Internationalists.'

The Reverend Paradise looked hurt. 'The Lord makes brothers of all men.'

'Yet you make the flag of the British Empire in your fireworks in the garden! If it had not been for your Union Jack our schoolhouse would still have windows!'

Now Ayres was interested. He looked from Willy, who had opened his mouth and frowned, as though he did not quite follow what she was saying, to the woman. She sat, with the anger still in her face, sensing her advantage but unsure about whether to press it. Ayres guessed this was not the first time the two missionaries had had disagreements.

'Then you are simply another kind of patriot,' Willy said. He asked her slyly, 'You support the aims of the Kuomintang, do you not?'

'What is required at the present time is a vigorous Chinese nationalism.' She was about to elaborate, but seemed to change her mind and sat back.

Julia watched them fiercely. Her small head flicked from her husband to the woman, then back again.

'Let me tell you something about patriotism,' Miss Platz said pleasantly to Willy. 'I lost my patriotic fervour at Oxford in 1916 when I was sent down without taking my degree.'

The three of them waited for her to continue. 'Oxford was a very quiet place during the war. You talk of patriotism—all the young men were enlisting. Intelligent boys, brilliant boys, eighteen, nineteen, they were only children. But I wasn't a child. I was twenty-three years old. The colleges were nearly empty. There were barracks and hospitals in the town. I did what I could for the war effort. It was not as though I was trying to remain neutral. I performed voluntary nursing duties at one of the hospitals. One night when I was walking home to my college I was attacked. A group of boys had been drinking. They held me down. Out came the predictable taunts. I was a Bosch, a Hun, an enemy. One of the boys tipped some stuff he was carrying in my hair. You know Stockholm tar? You know what it smells like? I complained to the authorities. An enquiry was held. My college decided that I should be the one to leave.'

A sudden look of doubt, almost of fear, came across her face when she saw Ayres watching her. She had spoken more than she needed to. Ayres slumped back in his chair, his cigar in his mouth, and said quietly, 'That must have been a very painful time, Miss Platz. You must find it difficult to talk about it.'

She smiled and Ayres saw that the corner of one of her front teeth was chipped. 'Not at all, *Doktor.*' She pronounced his honorific in the German manner, iron-

ically, making him feel uneasy, outwitted in some ob-
scure way. Partly it was her being German. The vague
idea floated through his mind that he wouldn't mind
asking what was her father's name.

'My hero,' Willy Paradise was saying to him. 'Is
Timothy Richard. You've heard of him?'

Ayres admitted that he had not.

'A very famous missionary indeed. The Chinese
called him Li-Ti-Mo-Tai. He had an extraordinary reputation in scholarly circles. Not everyone could accept
his methods, of course, least of all our more conven-
tional brethren. Timothy Richard dreamed of China
reforming herself, rather than of a country studded with
Western churches. He tried to emphasize the essentials
of Chinese culture in his teaching. He inspired many
young Chinese to join the revolutionary movement back
in those days. But he was convinced that China must
have Western learning. He lived in abject poverty, din-
ing on rice and vegetables so that he could buy tele-
scopes and microscopes for his students. And here we
are—look at us!—having dined on roasted pork.' He
looked at Ayres as though that were his fault.

'An excellent meal,' said Ayres. 'You met this man
Timothy Richard?'

'Sadly I never had the opportunity. He died in
1919. But he left his mark, my word he did. Now we
have the New Missionaries and their national salvation
through reform. That's Timothy's work. The *social* gos-
pel, as they now call it.'

'Those soldiers out there don't seem to appreciate it,'
Ayres said.

89

Julia said loudly, 'Of course they appreciate it. Didn't you see how it amused them to smash out our windows?' Then, more quietly, 'They were only being Chinese.'

Willy turned to Ayres, 'You have to understand that missionaries in this country have traditionally been targets for nationalist attacks. We have been extraordinarily lucky here. A handful of soldiers billeted for a few days. In a week or two our students will return. A few windows smashed. It would make your stomach turn to hear of some of the atrocious things that have been done to our people in the past.'

Julia said, 'Our girls will return if Johnny Yang will let them.'

'Who is he?' Ayres asked.

Willy said, 'One of the policemen at the prefecture. One of those who, as you say, doesn't seem to appreciate us. It's really all very petty. Occasionally a girl's family wants her back. They sign an agreement then two or three months later someone puts pressure on them, or they decide they're not Christians any more and they want them out. Sometimes they just send a few bully boys to get the girl back. Puts us in a terrible position. They might be abducting the girl, for all we know. It actually happened to one girl, last year. At other times they send young Captain Yang for them. A duty which, I might hasten to add, Captain Yang delights in performing.' Willy Paradise paused for a moment, as if deciding whether to go on. 'He hates us. Loathes us with a fine burning hatred. He believes it is his sacred duty to drive all Christians out of China.'

'But why send the police? Why not simply come and take the girl home themselves?'

Willy Paradise shrugged. 'Cowardice, I suppose.'

Julia said sharply, 'They are afraid Willy will talk them out of it. Willy can be very—convincing.'

Finally the party broke up and Ayres dragged himself upstairs to his room. He took off his shoes and jacket, lighted his pipe and lay back on the bed.

A high-pitched shriek cut through the night. Ayres shook himself awake and remembered where he was. The shriek died away and now he heard the excited babble of Chinese outside in the garden. And another sound that was unmistakable: the crackling of flames.

The little wooden schoolhouse was already well alight when Ayres got there. The fire cast bright wobbly shadows over the garden. Bits of timber lay flaming on the grass and he heard the sharp knock and hiss as the iron roof collapsed. Flames leapt out and caught on the overhanging branches. The soldiers were doing nothing to stop the fire. They looked on with interest from their huddled rucksacks and bedrolls and rifles. Willy Paradise ran to the pump and filled one of the metal buckets left there, but the heat of the fire was so intense that he could not get close enough to throw his water at the flames.

'Is everybody out of there?' Ayres yelled across to him. Willy looked confused, then, understanding, turned and yelled something in Chinese to the soldiers. They did not seem to understand Willy's Mandarin. They looked at each other, then back to Willy and smiled. One of the young soldiers, who had the beginnings of a straggling moustache, lifted a bottle of rice spirit to his lips and drank, then, staring into the fire, passed it on to the soldier standing next to him.

Something made Ayres look up. Julia was standing in one of the dormer windows. She was looking beyond him to the burning schoolhouse and in the firelight her face was exultant.

Half an hour later the building was a skeleton of blackened timber which smoked and smouldered but would not fall. The soldiers had withdrawn with their belongings to the group of garden sheds which had been jerrybuilt against the back fence. As they left, one of them—it was the young one with the moustache—lugged his kit and bedroll over to where Willy stood by himself and took something out from inside his pack and handed it to Willy apologetically. Ayres saw that it was a microscope.

Willy had shown no signs of moving away from the smouldering ruin when Ayres had retired. He continued to stand there, oblivious to Ayres' goodnight, surveying what was left of his school.

The next morning Ayres found him still in the garden. He lifted his head but did not say anything. He had apparently not left the spot all night and his hands, face and clerical collar were filthy with soot and ash.

The building was cold black rubble. Part of the charred frame had collapsed during the night and roof timbers hung down dangerously from what was left. Sheets of iron lay here and there on the grass and Ayres inspected the blackened objects Willy had salvaged—an iron desk frame, a broken wash bowl, burnt books strewn from a partly burnt cupboard. As Ayres walked around, his feet stirred up clouds of ash.

Ayres said, 'Did the soldiers tell you anything?'

'They left early this morning. Didn't you hear the lorry arrive?'

'No.'

'It was deliberate. There can be no doubt about it. Look over there.' He nodded in the direction of the rubble. Ayres could not see what he meant at first, then he saw a blackened gasolene can, the faint red imprint of the brand name just visible.

'It's an absolute outrage,' Ayres told him. 'You must telegraph the Consul immediately. You must lose no time. We'll have them reported to their superior officers.'

Willy Paradise did not even bother to answer. He seemed to have sunk into a black despair. Ayres felt a strong sensation that the man hated him. Then the clergyman recounted a story that had been told him in the night by some young men: Not long before the fire had broken out, a woman made her way from the mission buildings down towards the canal at the back, where she untied from the small landing platform there a wooden dinghy. It was a mild night and some of the young peasant boys who had come up to watch the fireworks stopped at that spot where the canal, due to a sluice-gate, becomes a wide deep pool.

Along the bank grew a few willows, and from one of these trees a rope had been attached, from which on hot summer afternoons after harvesting these same young men swung out over the canal and plunged down into the water.

The water was flowing quickly that night because the sluice had been opened by the local water warden. For some reason known only at City Hall in Shanghai, the warden opened the locks to flood the canals at night time. The boys watched the woman travel more and more quickly down the canal without apparent struggle in the powerful current. She rowed smoothly and well [she had been in the Women's Eight at Somerville, Willy pointed out], for all the world as though she were going for a bit of a Sunday trip in one of those boats they have next to the English tea gardens at the Racing Club in Shanghai. Minutes later, the sky behind the willows was shot full of flames and the screaming from the mission rent the air. None of them gave another thought to the woman. Out in the middle of the canal the current moved her quickly into the darkness, away from the firelight.

'Have you seen Julia?' Ayres asked him quietly. His face told him that he had. 'Is she—sleeping?'

'She's sleeping now.'

There was something horrible about the way he said it.

'What do you mean?' Ayres demanded.

'I sat up with her until the early hours. I was going to wake you, but—I'm accustomed to giving the injections myself.'

'You mean she was hallucinating again?'

'Oh yes. Dreadfully. She kept insisting that someone had been burnt in the fire. I spent the whole night sitting with her, trying to get straight in her poor mind what had really happened. The truth is that I don't really know, myself. None of us does. I kept going

through the simplest steps of logic, as though explaining
to a child, that there was not, could not have been, any
of the girls burnt in the school. She said she saw the
house burning, thick palls of smoke coming from the
upstairs windows. She said she saw flames up there,
even the sound of breaking glass. She said she heard a
girl screaming—perhaps she had in the panic confused
the soldiers yelling—' Willy Paradise looked at Ayres,
the exhaustion and terror finally breaking over his face.
'And then she insisted, absolutely insisted, that she had
seen a girl in a nightgown jump from the burning upstairs window onto the lawn below.'

There were no servants to be seen and Ayres had to
make his own breakfast. He prepared eggs, buttered
toast and brewed tea for himself. The stacked plates and
dishes were still unwashed in the cold little scullery. In
the diningroom the table was still exactly as they had
left it, with the partly eaten birthday cake and the stubs
of cigars. As soon as he had finished breakfasting he felt
for his pipe then sat back and let the rich, sweet-smell-
ing smoke unwind over the debris. He went through
to the sittingroom and picked up a week-old *South
China Daily News* with its stale stories of the big strikes
in Shanghai.

The sounds of cars arriving outside roused Ayres but
by the time he had hauled himself to the sittingroom
window only a wake of dust was left, rising lazily in the
late morning sunshine.

He found Julia in the garden sitting on the wooden
seat built around a peppercorn tree, engaged in earnest
conversation with a policeman. He was a very well-

dressed young Chinese policeman, to be sure—he wore a Western tie and vest and clean white shirtsleeves, and balanced on his knee a bowler hat—but he was unmistakably a policeman, nevertheless. His jacket was folded neatly across the passenger seat of his motor-car, a late American model. In the green lorry behind it two other policemen, sullen and bored, sat in the cabin on either side of Willy Paradise. He still wore his ruined clerical collar and he had not washed his face. He sat up there impassively, and the combination of the blackened face and the lorry made Ayres think of a coalminer. A few moments passed before Julia realized Ayres' presence; then she turned her head to him, her black hair gleaming in the sun.

'They've arrested Willy,' she said.

Ayres stood his ground and regarded the well-dressed policeman. Julia made an introduction and the Chinese insisted on shaking hands. His name was Johnny Yang, and he spoke good English with an American accent.

'He's been arrested on what charge?' Ayres asked mildly.

'No formal charge is required. Perhaps you have not heard? The supreme command of the National Peoples' Party has declared a state of martial law.'

Suddenly Ayres was furious. He spoke sharply, his voice not disguising his loathing. 'Except in the International Settlement.'

The Chinese looked at him pleasantly. 'Except in the International Settlement, of course.' He bowed to the Concession and went on smoothly. 'Nevertheless, the Sungchiang prefecture is not presently under the jurisdiction of the International Settlement. The Reverend Paradise has been detained in connection with a fire which occurred last night on Chinese property.'

The policeman smiled.

'Are you seriously trying to suggest that Mr Paradise tried to burn down his own mission school?'

'If he burned his own mission it would be of no concern to us. But this mission is now Chinese property by forfeit under proclamation by the Supreme Commander General Chiang Kai-Shek that all foreign mission schools must have Chinese principals.'

Ayres was silent. He looked at the policeman, then asked, 'And how long will he be detained?'

'As long as it takes for the facts to come to light.'

Julia said softly, 'Willy will be staying for a few days, I think.' She stood smiling stupidly, in her Sunday frock. Then she looked down and plucked at the fingers of her glove.

Johnny Yang turned again to Ayres. 'Are you staying here, Doctor, in any official capacity?'

Ayres said slowly, afraid of letting his anger show, 'I am staying here as a guest of the Reverend and Mrs Paradise.'

The policeman seemed satisfied. 'Well then.' He turned towards his car. 'Now you are staying as a guest of the Chinese people. I trust you will do your utmost to protect Chinese property from any further damage. By person or persons unknown.' He put his bowler hat on his head and opened the door of the roadster. Then Julia moved forward and touched the shiny green fender.

'Does it go fast?' she asked silkily, caressing the duco.

'Very fast,' the man assured her, taking off his hat again and scrutinizing her face. 'But I myself am a slow and careful driver.' He smiled and gave a rather pretentious half bow forward, mocking the western image of the oriental manner, perhaps. 'It was a present from my father. A wedding present,' he grimaced slightly, showing straight white teeth.

'Your father must be very well off to shower such presents upon his children.'

'One gift. Hardly a shower.' He looked to Ayres who was watching Julia. The colour had risen in her face and her little schoolmarm's mouth was shut tight. She was staring into Johnny Yang's face. No wonder he was embarrassed. He could not have returned such intense scrutiny politely. She was really inspecting him, as though he were a rarity, an oddity: his smooth dry sallow skin with the flattened out nose, a face apparently without a seam or join in it anywhere, topped by the thick black neatly brilliantined hair.

Julia said, then, 'He didn't do anything wrong, you know. He has no understanding of politics.'

The policeman now understood. He said as he got into the car, 'You mustn't worry. We'll be in touch. Tomorrow maybe.'

'Come to tea,' Julia said flatly as he started the motor. Then the car moved off followed at a distance by the lorry, with Willy Paradise, a willing martyr, in his blackened collar still sitting up in dignified silence.

As they rounded the bend in the drive, Ayres saw Gerthilde Platz in her trousers and man's broad-crowned hat straighten up. She watched the roadster and the lorry until they were out of sight, then turned back to pruning the roses.

Julia had put on the old cardigan again and she was smoking cigarettes one after the other. Ayres heard music coming from somewhere in the house, upstairs, he thought, the sound of a gramophone playing the same American jazz tune over and over again. He thought it extremely unlikely that Gerthilde Platz would be playing that kind of music.

Julia's face was screwed up as she spoke. She did not seem to have noticed the music. She was talking about her childhood with the old intensity. Her words, which had begun to slur, came out in venomous little bursts as she struggled for breath in the middle of sentences. Now and then she had to stop herself and make a loose sucking noise because of the saliva that had collected in her mouth. 'The first night Willy came to the Hotel Continental he was just another man in a suit who had come to pay to get rid of his excess fluids.' She suddenly looked very much older than her thirty-one years of age. Her eyes looked raw.

After a silence she spoke on, her voice ugly.

'Later that night I saw a man chasing the child along the balcony outside. She was terrified. I ran to the door but she was already at the end of the balcony, the man nearly with her. And then she turned and jumped. When I looked over the rail I could see her white night-dress spread out on the road below.'

Little claws of lines had crept around her mouth which she had rouged a shocking red since the afternoon.

'Tina Terrina put her big arms around me and wouldn't let me go down to look. We cried together in her bed all night. I can still feel her big breasts shaking in her nightgown.'

Visions of her past continued to pour out of Julia. Everything stubbornly and perversely failed to flesh out the Freudian bones of the 'case' assembled by Ayres in his clinical notes. As on their Tuesday afternoons she would brook no interruptions for question or clarification.

At one point, suddenly turning in her chair, she switched on the standard lamp and picked up from the floor a flat cardboard box and opened the lid. Still talking all the time, she began shuffling through the dozens of photographs inside. Ayres watched her with a foreboding that he was about to be shown her 'night pictures'.

It was dark outside and Ayres was anxious to get going. She was not capable of driving the motor-car and even if he could make it to the station there was no certainty that trains had not been delayed or even cancelled. He felt trapped. He wanted to stop the woman speaking because she was telling him things he did not want to hear, but there was a part of him sitting in that room, with Ayres but not of him, so it seemed, that cold cruel part of his mind which continued to listen behind the knocking of his heart. So excited was that scientific part of him that he said nothing, and sat and watched her hand shake as she lighted her next cigarette.

Open on the table beside his chair was the flat cardboard box of photographs. They had indeed proved to

be her 'night pictures' of the Chinese quarter in Shanghai: a legless beggar sitting on the footpath outside the
entrance of a bank; coolies carrying huge bales on either
end of bamboo poles bent over their backs; the girl-
prostitutes, scarcely twelve or thirteen, lifting their skirts
to expose themselves, hungry eyes grotesque above their
mannequins' figures; a man wearing a gas mask, and
behind him an open tray truck piled with corpses. There
were photographs taken in the early-morning tea shops
and around the markets, and none of them would have
seemed out of place in a police coroner's report. But the
subject of the photograph he was staring at was very
much alive: one of the waif-prostitutes with her gleaming hair piled up on top of her head, her blouse open
to reveal her unformed breasts, her face with its preco-
cious make-up pouting forward at the camera as though
she recognized some image in the lens, or behind it. It
was the girl called Lucy, whom Morgan McCaffrey had
hired as a model a couple of times and whom Ayres
himself had used occasionally.

Now Julia spoke urgently, and it was apparent to
Ayres that she was entrusting him with everything because she sensed she might be running out of time. She
was full of stories that afternoon, specific and detailed
as if they had actually occurred, a victim of her own
fiction. 'I didn't realize it was Lucy at first, with her face
painted. I had only seen her in her blue school tunic.
It had been six months. Even her family had given her
up for dead. I had loved that girl. She had been my
special girl, she was different from the others. I remem-
ber the first time she came to me and recited by heart,

In Xanadu did Kubla Khan
A stately pleasure-dome decree . . .'

Suddenly Julia looked up at him. 'You *killed* her,
Ayres.'

The face of the child looked back at him from the photograph. The door opens and the painter, Morgan, re-
mains at the easel. Behind his left shoulder Ayres can
see the girl. At the sound of the door closing she turns
and stares at him with such silent force that her head
is thrust forward and her naked body seems out of bal-
ance. Morgan, bearded, with unkempt hair, hardly even
European-looking in his padded blue coolie's jacket,
does not move at Ayres' intrusion. He stands impassively, his brush classically, almost pretentiously, poised
in the air. His look is stern, his beard and moustache
cover his mouth and any sign of emotion it might have
given away. Only the eyes are clear, blue, open, almost
transparent, giving him something of the piercing expression of the blind. When he finally speaks his voice
is playful, amused, out of keeping with that gruff out-
crop of beard. He says in his slow, amused voice, 'Well,
lookey me. If it isn't little Lucy's doctor friend here.
Whatever can he want?'

'I want you to show me the picture,' Ayres says.

Lucy's dark eyes look towards Ayres, then wander
around the room, unwilling to meet his gaze. It is a
large whitewashed room with a stone floor. The room
is barbarically bare: no mats, no carpets, no stove for
heat, and the model is shivering. Only the walls are
covered with Morgan's paintings, some on paper, others

on cardboard, plywood, the sides of a tea chest. In the middle of the room where he stands is the makeshift easel, the small work table, nothing more. Ayres looks around at the ten or twelve works pinned to the walls— teahouse scenes, lake scenes, boats drifting along a canal, strangely large brownskinned native women with egg-like breasts seabathing.

The painter watches him, his blue eyes still smiling. 'Well, missee,' he says. 'Well, little Lucy. We'd better find out what little Lucy's friend the doctor wants. You want to know what he wants, don't you, missee?'

She whimpers and stares hard at Morgan: intense, her fragile body twisting away, dark eyes shining, a tiny forest animal that might break its cover and run. He laughs sympathetically and takes Ayres by the shoulder, 'Come on, little Lucy's friend. Come into the warm. We wouldn't want you to wear out your big bad bear's feet, now would we?'

He opens the door into the next room. The girl hesitates, then scampers through under his arm. He closes the door of his icy studio gently behind them. They are in a smaller room, almost as bare, but the warmth from the squat porcelain stove in the corner and the furled bed mat make the room feel less stark. A small window high up lets the bleak northern light into the room and shows up the large picture resting against a wall. On canvas this one, and still on its stretchers: a nude of the twelve-year-old girl. Ayres is not prepared for this cold realism, the girl's flat breasts with the nipples scarcely formed, the childish paunch of her belly, no less than the surprise of her pubic hair. There is a message written clearly in the drooping languorous lines of her body, her lank blue-black hair which hangs as though sodden with sweat, the tousle of the bed mat in the background, this same bed mat now rolled up against the wall: Morgan has captured there the sadness of a man's receding desire, a desire not entirely satisfied, and on the girl's face, the despair of repeated rape. Ayres waits and watches for little Lucy's reaction, which does not come. Then the suddenness and force of his movement makes her cry out as he bends her forward against the wall. As he fumbles with his trouser buttons the sadness and the pity of it sticks in his throat.

In another country, and besides, the wench is dead, he thought. What difference between a ruptured uterus and a perforated rectum when a girl dies in the streets. The man from City Hall with the gas mask and the open truck wouldn't stop to find out. Or perhaps she had been picked up from the gutter by a woman who haunted the night streets in an old raincoat and scarf, with a camera, and taken to a missionary hospital to do her dying under a cross. Now, sitting in Julia's living-room with the burden of the minutes ticking through his nerves, he could do nothing but wait for Julia to tell him.

He would relive for a long time everything she said in the room at the mission. He would recall the way her voice had grown thicker and thicker, and how her head had begun to hang to one side from the exhaustion of her telling, and how, the second time he had made himself face the photograph of the dead child, Julia had looked up and said, 'That first Tuesday I came to your bed, I wanted to know what kind of man could do that.'

Willy Paradise was a small fish swimming in a dangerous stretch of ocean, as the First Secretary, Gerald Cole, pointed out to Ayres in the Long Bar. He would see what he could do, but really what was the point of a diplomatic Note, except to give some Chinaman a laugh, when it was taking every British and American marine available to keep the Nationalist troops out of the Settlement? So Willy Paradise simply disappeared.

Several months later Ayres visited the actual building on the outskirts of Shanghai where the Nationalist secret police had kept their headquarters. It was a derelict grim-looking house with an overgrown garden behind a high stone wall. He peered through the empty doors and windows. There was simply nothing to see; certainly not Willy's ghost, even if Willy had been taken there. There were several small rooms in the cellar, but no blood, no human feces, no hint as to what purposes they had served. He climbed the rickety stairs to an attic room whose window looked down onto the garden at the back, also full of weeds. He saw the brick wall with the three whitish patches where the bricks and cement had been chipped away. He went down the stairs and into the sunshine for a closer look.

The white patches had been chipped away by bullets. He could see where the prisoners would have stood, three at a time, facing the wall. Then the volley of bullets. The holes in the wall were deep: the process had been repeated hundreds of times. He worked his way back to where the executioners would have stood. Hundreds of bullet cases littered the ground under the weeds. The brass cases glittered in the sun.

Ayres looked around him. Behind the wall were telegraph poles, an ordinary thatched bamboo garden fence, roofs of houses. The noises of the morning drifted into the derelict garden, the everyday cheerful neighbourhood noises of voice and car and rooster. The perfect ordinariness of the morning the other side of that garden wall hurt him. He realized that he hated China almost as much as he hated life. Shanghai was, after all, a detour he had never intended. For years now, he had been holed up in this sordid stopping-off place. His home was still a hotel. He felt that he had lived for nearly thirty-five years in this world and he had understood nothing. And something else: he felt that he had failed to understand the import of Julia Paradise's gift to him.

She was like a brilliantly coloured jigsaw puzzle dismantled and spread across the floor of his mind. His thoughts continued to inhabit small sections of her life— or what he increasingly thought of as her 'lives'. He talked aloud to her, pleading with her to clarify this point, to explain the apparent contradiction between this and that to make sense of the brutal pantomime he played over and over. In short, he became obsessed.

Even in the Master he found only discouragement. Freud himself had written, 'It still strikes me myself as strange that the case histories I write should read like short stories . . .' And from his own lecture notes of 1919: 'Psychoanalysis is in essence a cure through love.' Ayres thought of his own inability to love. Could he aspire to being no more than a helpless voyeur into the lush interiors of women? He felt that his training, his scientific method, had failed him.

He seemed always to be hungry, even after a big meal; but his hunger was a restlessness which raged through his nerves, so that in the evenings he had to get out of doors and walk the streets, and he found his footsteps always leading in the same direction . . . there was nothing else for it but to pursue her in the thin ghostly figures of the girls, who either turned to him openly with painted smiles, or who fled from him down the unlit streets. He shivered when he remembered certain parts of her 'telling' and he felt sudden fierce desires to walk down Bubbling Well Road to find such a one who might initiate him again into the mysteries, with the river lapping, the parrots shrieking, and with the overpowering scent of the eucalypts. But no matter how often he took their little bodies, he remained excluded from the world of the Duck River.

He sought out the Australian foreign correspondent who drank at the Long Bar. '*Duck* River, you say—' The man looked hard back at Ayres, then shook his head. 'Sorry, old man.'

Then, out of the blue, the following year she telephoned him at the Astor House Hotel. Could she see him? That afternoon? In front of the post office in Szechuan Road at five o'clock?

Ayres left the hotel early, before four. It was a bright summer's afternoon outside with a delicious soft sea wind. There were several empty rickshaws pulling up Szechuan Road but he decided instead to walk. The prospect of seeing Julia again excited him. A sudden happiness filled him, and he realized how deliberately he had been trying to wean himself off the thought of her. He got there exactly as the post office clock struck five.

Julia was already waiting. He barely recognized her. She looked much better. Her eyes still had that excessively tired look of the habitual narcotics user but now, he saw in the sunlight, she had exaggerated the effect with mascara and kohl. She had put rouge on her lips and her cheeks looked healthy, blooming. Ayres could tell straight away that she had come to rely less heavily on morphine.

But she wore her heavy overcoat against the clear, hot day and had the same silk scarf knotted over her hair. 'No news of Willy?' Ayres asked her immediately. She looked back at him, almost uncomprehending. He hailed a taxi and took her straight to Delmonico's for something to eat.

When they were inside the restaurant Julia took off her coat and scarf. He was surprised at her fashionable dress. The skirt ended just below the knee and the sleeveless bodice was deeply bloused over the hipband. She wore a long string of pearls around her neck. Her hair had been cut recently, too, bobbed short in the new American style, which caused the Europeans at the other tables to turn around and look at her.

'I need money,' she said straight away when he had ordered.

'I'm surprised you haven't asked me for it sooner.' She looked away. 'How much?' he asked.

'A lot.'

'How much is a lot? Ten pounds? Twenty?'

'I need a hundred and sixty-five English pounds,' she said seriously.

'I can't lay my hands on that amount at a moment's notice.'

'You haven't got it?' There was a teasing tone in her voice, the irony and self-loathing of the blackmailer.

'I've got it, of course. It's just that I'll need a couple of days to put my hands on it. I shall have to draw a draft on my bank.' Ayres knew that he could walk into his bank at ten o'clock the next morning and be given the notes, but he wanted time to decide if she really needed it. And whether *he* needed to give it to her. He said, 'You're not pregnant?'

'Not pregnant.'

'Is it political?'

She shook her head.

'Where are you living?'

'In the Concession. I'll give you the address later.'

'You're staying with friends?'

'No,' she said quietly. 'In a boarding house.'

He looked at the tired, black-rimmed eyes, and a sudden thought struck him. 'Where are you getting your supplies of morphine?'

'I'm all right.' After a moment she added, 'Thank you.'

'This boarding house. Is it the kind of place I might want to visit?' Her eyes watered and her cheeks reddened so suddenly she might have just been slapped across the face. She did not answer, so he said, 'Why do you need the money?'

She started to speak, then took a little breath, and said in a quiet, dignified voice, 'We are going abroad. We are going to live in Germany.'

'We? A man?'

She shook her shorn head and said quietly, 'I am not going to continue to live in this country. A man has arranged passage for us on a liner leaving at the end of the month. But I have to find a hundred and sixty-five pounds to pay him.' She had said all this looking down at the table top, touching the saucer, the teapot, the half-eaten cake on the plate in front of her. She looked up and said quickly, 'Can I have a cigarette?'

The simplicity of her request moved him, and he raised his hand for the waiter. He knew then he would give her the money. She said, 'There's one last thing I have to ask. I want you to visit Gertie . . .'

The address she had given him was a run-down two storey house in the American Concession. It was in fact in Szechuan Road, directly opposite the post office where he had met Julia the previous afternoon. Their rooms were on the upper floor, above a brothel. The small garden at the front was overgrown and most of the mosaic tiles on the front porch had been chipped away through neglect. The front door was open and as he walked down the passage a door on his left opened and a man looked at him, a smiling Chinese in his late forties, with brilliantined hair and a dirty yellow shirt collarless and open at the neck.

Their rooms were surprisingly spacious. There was a window overlooking the Soochow Creek. Gerthilde

Platz received him alone. The door through to the bed-room was shut and he wondered if Julia was in there. His former impression of the German woman was re-inforced by the clothes she wore: the same dark, shape-less woollen suit, although he noticed the silver crosses were gone. He saw that her head had been close-cropped like Julia's. She smiled and shook hands with him. By the window she had set up a low tea table with a damask cloth with her books, notebooks and pens laid out, and a couple of wicker chairs with soft cushions. On the window ledge she had several small potted plants grow-ing towards the light. The room had the austere feel of a cloister, and on the wall she had tacked cheap litho-graphic poster-pictures of her three saints: Marx, Engels and Lenin.

She said in her rich, rounded accent, 'I'm afraid I don't know where to start. The fact is that we have been less than entirely honest with you.'

He sat in one of the wicker chairs and took the brown envelope with the hundred and sixty-five pounds out of his coat pocket and put it on the table in front of her. She looked down at it, not betraying any satisfaction she might have felt. Then she opened the flap of the en-velope, which he had not sealed, and began counting out the wad of ten and five pound notes.

'Forgive me,' she said. 'It is important. I think you do not lead so sheltered a life that you have not heard what they are doing to communists here.'

He looked at the titles of the few books and pam-phlets lying closed on her table: *Materialism and Empirio-Criticism*; *Reform or Revolution*; *Die Krise der Sozialdemocratie*; 'One Step Forward, Two Steps Backward'; a tattered German edition of *Das Kapital*. He looked down at the open page of her diary half-filled with her spidery black handwriting. He wondered what had happened to Willy's manuscript on the propagation of Pacific coral . . .

'You know the word *Heizer?*' he asked her.

She looked up from the half-counted banknotes with shock on her face. 'Julia told you *that?*'

He nodded.

For the first time since Ayres had met her she looked embarrassed. 'A private term. How shall I put it—"One who makes the fires?"' With a slight sweep of the back of her hand she indicated the lower part of her body. 'I thought you knew about Julia and me, you see. I thought you knew about us before we went to Hangchow. Yes, Hangchow,' she smiled. 'The mountains, the lake. But we did not go there to take the *air*. We went to hear Michael Borodin speak to a meeting of comrades.'

'And the other fire?'

She looked at him for a moment as though she did not understand. 'You were under instructions?' Ayres pressed her. 'Those soldiers *were* coming to break the general strike.'

She said quietly, 'No, I hadn't planned it, if that's what you mean. I can't tell you why I did it.'

'Spontaneous combustion,' sneered Ayres.

'Spontaneous. You Freudians are even less comfortable with that word than we are ourselves. Let's just call it an "infantile disorder". Do you know Lenin?'

'No,' he said.

'A shame. You should read him.' She went on more

brightly, 'You might as well also know that she told Paradise. Not only about *us*. About you.'

'The night of the fire.'

The woman nodded curtly, once.

'She might have chosen a better time!'

'She wanted to hurt him as little as possible. But you have not come here for me to trade recriminations. I have asked you to come because I want your help.'

'If you want more money—'

The woman held up her hand. 'No, no. I want to ask your advice on a medical matter.'

'An examination.'

'Just so.' She smiled grimly and nodded, and continued to nod to herself after she had spoken, as if to put off the moment of her next action. Then she stood and began to unbutton her shirt. The weals of her skin disease stood out clearly in the light from the window. Her skin was discoloured from the area between the left breast and the armpit down along the side of the stomach. The colour was deep brown in patches, in others the yellow or tawny colour of a lion's skin. Near the armpit the weals and nodules of cutaneous thickening appeared.

'Hansen's Disease,' said Ayres. 'Leprosy.'

She nodded back at him with the same ironic smile.

Ayres said, 'You've had it treated? Hansen's Disease can be mildly contagious.'

'What about treatment?'

'Isolation. There are leprosaria for the purpose.'

'Drugs?'

'Chaulmoogra oil has been used in the past. Nowadays many people question its value.'

'Life expectancy?' she demanded.

'Ten years. Perhaps longer if secondary infection doesn't set in.'

'Can Julia get it?'

He regarded her watchfully for a moment. 'She could.'

'Then isolation it is,' she said, nodding. She buttoned her shirt and sat down again. 'My political work in Germany will have to wait.' She sat and looked out the window for a while at the hundreds of sampans crammed in at odd angles along the bright, straw-coloured water of the Soochow Creek. 'Are there leprosaria in Australia?' she asked.

'My good woman, I don't even know where Australia is.'

She smiled at him.

'Oh yes,' she said. 'Julia wants you to have these.' She reached down to the floor under the table and handed him the cardboard box of photographs.

'Julia is really very much better. There is still the morphine, but I hope to wean her off that slowly. The fact is that when she came to you she was broken to pieces. She is strong now, really strong. Her will is strong.' She was smiling that same knowing smile again. Ayres looked into her face and it always seemed to him afterwards that he had been looking into the face of the future, the face of the twentieth century.

Ayres saw that sure face many times during the next twenty years in China. He saw her in the faces of the peasants, workers and soldiers as they joined the struggle. In his old age, on quiet mornings in his flat in

Princes Street in Edinburgh, he would think back to that face and ascribe to it all that happened, all that he saw as he followed the battle fronts north and south with his temporary field hospital, the old Bedford truck he had converted into an ambulance.

All this did not happen suddenly, of course. He remained as aloof from the world as ever through the rest of that year as Chiang Kai-Shek's purges of the communists spread from Shanghai to other regions under conservative commanders, and Borodin and the other Russian advisers were sent packing back to Moscow. He could still remain detached from the stories he perused in the *South China Daily News* of Chinese Communists being hunted down and executed in ordinary gardens in ordinary towns with telegraph poles and chicken runs and the whoops of playing children and patches of chipped brickwork on garden walls . . .

He found himself smoking more opium, sometimes six and seven pipes a night. But the relaxation they produced brought not soothing dreams but a power and clarity of imagination that allowed him again to inhabit Julia's 'region'. And no amount of the drug could relieve the tense, unpleasant beating of his heart.

Nor did it happen the next year, as the Nationalist army advanced north, inciting the people against the Christian churches and hospitals and schools, and the propaganda posters went up on the walls of Shanghai, bizarre as something out of Julia's 'childhood':

The foreign devils worshipping the Pig. Beating the foreign devils and burning their books. The Practitioners of the Grunt of the Pig removing the fetus.

The terrible punishment of Christ, the Pig Incarnate. Only after seeing the saws cutting, the pestles pounding, the cauldrons boiling and the grindstones grinding in dark Hell's eighteen levels, will the foreign devils know. You who in this world have committed a thousand times ten thousand crimes, who have castrated boys, removed the fetuses from pregnant women, gouged out people's eyes, and cut off women's nipples. . . . After we have pierced the Pig's body with ten thousand arrows will the monster again dare to grunt?*

Nor did the Mukden Incident and the Japanese invasion of Manchuria or the stories of the horrors there move Ayres, at first. All that existed only to fill the columns of the *South China Daily News* and the *Shanghai Evening Post*, where Ayres caught the snippet that Generalissimo Chiang Kai-Shek, now married to one of the Soong sisters, had converted to Methodism.

In the Shanghai Club in the International Settlement life went on much the same as ever. Businessmen were a little more touchy about the world Depression, perhaps; Englishmen's wives continued tiredly to pine for home; their daughters continued to pick their marks in the colonial service and when their best shots fell short, became temporarily hysterical or fell into a profound malaise. For Ayres, business was slightly better than usual, if anything.

He still found himself eagerly 'eavesdropping' on the private worlds of women. Perhaps a line, a word under hypnosis would excite his imagination in the old way

* The Chinese character for pig is homophonous for Lord.

. . . but there was nothing. He became more harsh and ironic with his patients. He had lost faith in his calling, in the whole scientific approach of psychoanalysis.

He still presented himself at the Long Bar early each afternoon and after luncheon retired upstairs to smoke in the reading room, that wonderful cocoon of quiet contentment in a city of jangled nerves. There, 'boys' in white jackets with brass buttons appeared as if by intuition when it was time for another brandy, there were deep leather armchairs and green-shaded reading lamps and the air was soft and spicy with cigar smoke and one could safely expect to meet men of comfortable opinions.

It was there, sunk deep in his chair in the quiet gloom of shuttered daylight, Ayres overheard a British naval Commander who had recently come down from Manchuria telling another man—'War's a nasty business, all right.' Ayres stifled a yawn and turned back to his newspaper.

'One thing in particular . . . the Japs herded together all the Chinese children in one village and systematically punctured their ear-drums . . .'

Ayres heard the words spoken, just like any other words of a gruesome century. The moment passed, the naval Commander left. Soon it would be time to head for home.

But the simple horror of it stayed with Ayres, and in the taxi on the way back to the Astor House he could still picture the uniforms and the Japanese officers' caps, the fixed bayonets and the little bundle of thin bamboo skewers—and suddenly his cheeks were wet and he was struggling for breath. He took out his bandana handkerchief and covered his face, wiped the perspiration from the edges of his beard, looked around. The driver had not noticed.

In his rooms at the Astor House that night he took out the box of Julia's photographs from where it had lain all this time in a cupboard. He looked through them until he came to a certain face. The eyes looked back at him frankly, even curiously, but without accusation. He recognized the street where the photograph had been taken. It was still the same. He walked down there sometimes. It was still haunted by the little ladies, just as much a part of Shanghai as the sampans in the Creek, the cranes on the skyline, further out the ships riding at anchor. He remembered the first morning he had disembarked in 1922 and melted into the city, anonymous, free. Now this face in the photograph looked across history and recognized him.

Later that month, in February 1932, the Japanese bombed the Chinese quarter of Shanghai and the barbed-wire barricades went up on streetcorners. In March an agreement was signed to cease hostilities around Shanghai, but Ayres' decision had already been made. He had used medicine as an escape before, so why not again? That same month he tidied his affairs and quit his rooms at the Astor House Hotel. He took the train to Peking, huddled in a cold third class compartment without blankets, unheard of for a European.

He leased the servants' compound of a Chinese house on the outskirts of the old Tartar City and there, amongst the shrieks and brays and family quarrels, he commenced his practice. He made beds from scavenged mattresses; his operating table was converted from kitchen uses. He secured pharmaceuticals and other medical supplies with the aid of the local bishop and the English-woman whose little auxiliary liaised with the International Committee of the Red Cross in Shanghai. He made do with whatever materials he could get his hands on; but always there was opium. He charged a fee only of those who could afford it: there was the small inheritance from his father at his bank in Shanghai; somehow he managed to make do. On Sundays he packed the contents of his medical bag into a rucksack and took long walks outside the city walls, followed channels towards the hill towns, stopping along the way wherever he was needed. He was drawn further and further into the countryside . . .

Camels were still common in that quarter of Peking and he conceived the idea of travelling by camel into the Interior; but with the help of the bishop he secured instead a Bedford truck, which he converted to an ambulance with plywood sides. It took him several weeks to learn how to drive—he had never driven even a motor-car before—and he was the object of amusement and the cause of not a little alarm as he practised, crunching the gears, tooting and reversing up the dusty roads outside the city wall, the little English bishop jumping up and down in the passenger's seat beside him, urging him on.

Thus began his series of slow, circuitous journeys which took him through many regions of northern China, ministering to the sick in the back of his truck or in the hospital tent which was sometimes pitched for weeks at a time in the more isolated towns. The Chinese say that a devil must walk a straight line, but the routes Ayres took criss-crossed, forked, and wound back upon themselves, so that if they had been drawn on a map they would have formed a kind of cat's cradle over northern China. He referred to his map only to calculate distances to towns for petroleum, and every few months he turned up in Peking for medical supplies, to fill his fifteen fuel cans, to stock up on food and tobacco. But mainly he travelled without maps, relying on word of mouth to tell him where he was needed.

He became known through vast tracts of the north, but not in a run of syllables like other foreigners revered by the Chinese—Li-Ti-Mo-Tai or Ma-Li-Sun. He was known simply as Ayres—'es' they pronounced it. 'Ayres will be here next week' or 'They say Ayres is in Honan, where there is a smallpox outbreak.'

Sometimes he travelled in convoy with other volunteers; at other times, stuck on a roadside with a broken axle or cut off by flood, he was so lonely he heard himself speaking to the spider which lived in a cobweb in the corner of the windscreen.

His beard went prematurely grey. He took to wearing slender, wire-rimmed spectacles, a leather aviator's helmet with ear flaps against the cold, a quilted blue coolie's jacket . . . gradually he got his tongue around the dialects.

The Communists completed their Long March to northern Shensi; Ayres was there for a time. He travelled through the Japanese-held regions of Manchuria and in 1937, when the war broke out in earnest, he followed the battle fronts north and south, now with the official Red Cross emblem on the sides and roof of his truck. On several occasions he was strafed by Japanese air attack, the bullets splintering the plywood.

After taking Shanghai, the Japanese forces moved westward by river, land and air. Ayres saw gangs of civilians roped together and machine-gunned by the Japanese for sport. He witnessed shocking crimes committed against women. When the Japanese took a town, not even the very young or very aged escaped violation; then they were ruthlessly bayonetted.

Curiously, the Japanese showed no interest in Ayres. In one town he sat on a wall, smoking, while the shells burst around him; in a very real sense he 'walked among the dead'. In his foolhardy exploits he sought the death he had so earnestly desired, but it was Ayres' predicament in those years to be condemned to life. . . . With his motley Red Cross unit he followed the battle fronts in the Siang river valley; north of the Yangtze; in Shensi, west of the Yellow River; in the mountains of western Hunan.

In the permanent war that was China in those years he saw Gertie's face in the pestilence, famine and filth, in the open graves with hundreds of bodies when Ayres himself had to use a gas mask; in the devouring of girl-children in besieged towns; in the riots and tramplings when rice relief arrived.

Once in Hsuchow during the Civil War he arrived at a local hospital where every patient was dead. They had been left in their beds and starved when the hospital staff had retreated. The building was perfectly cold and silent and at that moment, too, he had thought of her face.

By the end he welcomed the victory of the Red Army,

if for no other reason than it would put an end to the suffering; so it was her face, and not her politics that he blamed.

War took away Ayres' interest in food and he even became resigned to smoking the harsh local tobacco in his pipes. On his brief returns to Shanghai he stocked up on the luxury of tins of Gallaher's Honeydew from British diplomats. He remained celibate all that time although there was a Christian Chinese nurse he worked with for a while named, improbably, Florence, whom he privately loved. He got out in 'forty-nine, in the month of the lull, on the Dutch luxury-liner *Boissevain,* and jostled in the customs shed with the rich Chinese, the Jews, the White Russians, the pimps and gangsters and Filipino dance bands. Eventually he returned to his birthplace to live in retirement in his flat in Princes Street.

Julia Paradise was lost somewhere in all that. He received several letters from her on his returns to Shanghai. Perhaps there are letters being forwarded somewhere in China still from the Astor House Hotel. Her letters addressed him in warm terms and described her dull life as a schoolmistress in a country parish in Australia. Ayres really had no idea why she had written, for she had nothing to tell him, or if she did she did not include any of it in her letters. They were precisely the kind of letters one might write to a distant rich uncle, unconvincing. They bore no relation to that distant time when she drifted with Joachim through the raucous river birds, when ferns grew eyes and moved. But he continued to float in that boat, trapped in her experience. Once initiated into that malevolent zoöptic universe there was no escape for Ayres. He believed stubbornly that if he could read deeply enough between the lines of those bland letters he would find those mythical animals still lurking somewhere. In an essential way he had never passed beyond that first Tuesday when she had initiated him. The jungle had spread over him, crowding out the sky, the thick green branches and vines brushing the boat, the surface of the Duck River lit by the brilliant green scum of vegetation. Was it so surprising that now he found her present world rather unreal? Julia's magical neurosis remained a mystery. His own words came back to him. 'The East . . . the solution is sometimes as simple as a steamship ticket home . . .'

And, as in life, the mysteries remained, became subterranean and mapped out only in his dreams. Ayres never heard of Morgan McCaffrey again. He had the occasional pipedream of migrating to Australia, but he relegated that to the realms of the imaginary, the mythic. He knew he would only be disappointed to find the real Mem, if it existed. He examined maps in the university library in Edinburgh, though, without result.

Slowly, even China faded, although the words Duck River puzzled the gum-chewing nurse in 1950 who heard him mutter them on his dying breath. Before he died Ayres had begun to dream of forest fires, of girls in white nightgowns leaping from burning windows. It wasn't Dante's hell he dreamed of. He was in a dry mud-coloured country, infested with eucalypts. Julia was there. And Gertie. The great trees each with a swooping sigh became burning torches, beacons in the night.

ABOUT THE AUTHOR

ROD JONES was born in 1953 and studied History and English at the University of Melbourne. Since graduating in 1976 he has been writing fiction and working at a variety of jobs, mainly teaching. He lives in the Victorian fishing and resort town of Queenscliff. This is his first book.